The Halfwit Halfling

By J Pal

Copyright © 2020 J Pal

All rights reserved.

The characters and events portrayed in this book are fictitious. Any similarities to real persons, living or dead, are coincidental and not intended by the authors.

No part of this book may be reproduced, or stored in a retrieval system, or transmitted in any form or by any means, electronic, mechanical, photocopying, recording, or otherwise, without express written permission of the publisher.

ISBN-13: 9798679998902

Table of Contents

Chapter 1 1

Chapter 2 9

Chapter 3 17

Chapter 4 25

Chapter 5 33

Chapter 6 41

Chapter 7 47

Chapter 8 53

Chapter 9 59

Chapter 10 65

Chapter 11 71

Chapter 12 79

Chapter 13 87

Chapter 14 95

Chapter 15 101

Chapter 16 109

Chapter 17 117

Chapter 18	125
Chapter 19	133
Chapter 20	141
Chapter 21	149
Chapter 22	155
Chapter 23	161
Chapter 24	171
Chapter 25	179
Chapter 26	187
Chapter 27	195
Epilogue	203

Chapter 1
The Price of Scritches

"I got cheesy chips with gravy!" I yelled, entering the apartment.

The smell of chicken gravy melting cheddar had me salivating. Now, authentic poutine will outshine the cheap takeout in my arms any day. The factory-made, processed cheddar had flour mixed in to prevent sticking and couldn't hold a candle to cheese curds. The former melts part way when exposed to heat and maintains its texture while the latter turns into chalky lava with a penchant for stringy messiness.

When sober, I'd never indulge in the cheap gravy they used. Machine-made granules brought shame to real gravy: plenty of onions, beef bones and red wine. It's easy to make and inexpensive, but I wouldn't expect kebab shops to waste their time or workforce on it. If the head chef at my part-time job saw me indulging in the drunken university student delicacy, judgement would be passed.

"Why aren't you at work?" my flatmate asked, cracking his door open. "Ahmed will be pissed if you're late on rent again."

"That happened once, a year ago!" I rolled my eyes. "Do you want cheesy chips or not?"

"Seriously, why aren't you at work?" he asked again, shakily. I knew something was wrong then; Louis rarely spoke to me in such a tone.

"The restaurant cancelled my shift," I told him. "I've been taking on too many hours, and the other cooks complained. So, I went down to the pub for open mic night. Six pints later and here I am."

"Wouldn't have hurt to let me know." Louis's guilty eyes glanced at the door behind me.

Damn it. Turning on my heel, I marched into the kitchen, and as expected, an utter disaster presented itself before me.

"You promised you'd sort it out this morning! This is your mess, Louis. You can't expect me to clean up behind you constantly."

"I was going to do it before you got home," he said in protest.

"Bullshit!" I placed the cheesy chips with gravy on the counter. "I heard you talking to your mum this morning. She's picking you up at eight, taking you home for the weekend. I know your tricks, mate. You were going to leave me here playing maid again!"

"I wasn't—"

"Don't give me that crap," I said, staring at the towering stack of plates and grease stained countertop loaded with rubbish, knowing full well he'd never get it done in half an hour. "Let's just do it together. That way I can make sure you don't hide dirty pans on the top shelves again."

That's right. Standing half a foot taller than me, he'd tried that on more than one occasion. Sneaky dickhead.

"Fine." His shoulders slumped in defeat. I knew it wouldn't be the last time he did it.

Working in a kitchen, I preferred keeping things hygienic and orderly. For the past three days, I'd attended early morning classes while working graveyard shifts. So, it had just been Louis eating and making a mess of our apartment. We'd been great friends during our first year of university, so, when moving out of the uni halls, we'd decided to get an apartment together. Unfortunately, things fell apart during our time living under the same roof.

"You get started on the dishes, and I'll take the bin out," I told him, "then we'll eat the chips and finish up."

Louis looked at me, eyebrows raised. "You mean you're still willing to share?"

"Of course. You might be an asshole, but we're still friends."

"How was the open-mic?" he asked, his face breaking into a wide smile.

"Shit," I answered. "People kept requesting Wonderwall. I only managed to get one song in."

"Fuck, Wonderwall."

"Fuck Wonderwall, indeed."

Chuckling to himself, he got to work scrubbing away at the plates. I knew Louis wasn't a bad guy. Just as lazy as they came. If I didn't push him to go food shopping with me once a week, he'd starve himself. Something was *seriously* wrong with the guy.

After wrestling the black plastic bag out of the bin, I spotted the leak dripping on the floor. The smart thing to do would've been to put it down and double bag it, but I panicked upon seeing the foul juices drip onto my new shoes. With my guitar on my back, I sprinted out of the ground floor apartment. On entering the alley behind the building, I punted the bag into the massive, brown dumpster.

Good. Finally, I could indulge in my favourite drunken craving. Breathing in the cold evening air, I turned back towards the door, when a little hiss made me jump. I had almost stepped on a small, orange cat.

"Where did you come from?" I asked, expecting it to run away now that it had survived my blue Converse, but the feline stood its ground. The little pussycat had mostly orange fur with white bits around its paws. It stared straight into my eyes as if issuing a challenge. "What do you want? Scritches?"

I kneeled down and offered it my hand. Watching it sniff my fingers brought back memories of Samantha. She and I had not long broken up. Strange how I missed her cats more than the person. Thinking of her only brought back images of her straddling her best guy friend at our Christmas party and a little bit of rage, but I still loved her kitties.

A smile spread across my lips when the little feline stepped into my reach. I knew what that meant. She'd permitted me to provide worship through pets and scritches. After several reprimanding smacks and bites, I had learnt where to stroke and where not to: the hallowed sweet spots.

So, I started at the middle of her back. Good. The cat leaned into my strokes. I was doing it! Three months since I last saw Samantha and I finally got the chance to touch a cat.

Sure, the cheesy chips and gravy were getting cold, but I wanted some more of this feline love; needed it. Would Louis mind if I took her inside? She didn't have a collar and I worried she might freeze in case it snowed. Yes. That excuse would work. Liverpool did get snow in March. Occasionally.

"I'm going to call you Boots," I said, moving on to scritch her between the ears. The cat closed its eyes and purred. Man, I missed that sound. When I picked her up, she didn't panic.

Feeling pleased with myself, I walked up the stairs to the back door and let myself in. Huh? The lights had gone out.

"Louis! Is it the fuse again?" I asked.

No response. Instead, I heard a thunderous cheering all around me.

"Louis?"

〖Welcome, Earthling!〗

I almost jumped out of my skin when a blue screen popped up in front of my eyes.

〖Miss Purrfect, Herald to the Devourer of Worlds, has picked you as the next champion for the Games〗

"What the hell is this?" I asked out loud. "Did I slip and hit my head?"

〖No. You're in the Cosmic Horror Gambling Association, the leading venue for viewing and betting in Game World! You should be proud! Please wait for your future patron deity, The Devourer of Worlds, to grace you with her presence〗

"This isn't real." Carrying Boots in my left hand, I pressed the right to my chest. Why wasn't my heart racing? More importantly, why couldn't I feel my heart beating. "Is this some kind of joke? Louis what's going on? Are you hotboxing again? You know I can't handle the shit you smoke—"

I froze when a me-high pillar of golden light blinked into existence. Trying to shield my eyes, I almost dropped Boots. Meowing angrily she dug her claws into my arm and moved onto my shoulder. That should have hurt more. I felt her do it, but it didn't hurt. I wasn't a religious man, but I'm sure no faith mentioned an afterlife like this one.

"This is a dream, right?" I asked. "That's why it doesn't hurt."

"Miss Purrfect, not again!" the light exclaimed in a shrill female voice, snapping me to attention. "You're such an asshole! Why do you keep doing this to me? I just managed to convince the other dickheads to let the last guy in, and you bring another."

Surprised, I looked at it directly and realised it wasn't a pillar. A woman made of blinding white light stood before me. Samantha would never hold a candle to her literally or figuratively. The phrase blindingly beautiful must have been coined for her.

Boots—Miss Purrfect meowed defiantly, leaping off my shoulders. She looked between the woman who blazed like starmatter and me. Hold on a second. *Cosmic Horrors*? Were we in outer space? Come to think of it, I didn't smell anything anymore. Now that I thought about it, I wasn't breathing either.

"Don't take that tone with me! What am I supposed to do with him?" A game-like tag appeared above the woman's head.

〖The Devourer of Worlds〗

"Do you know how much I'll lose if they find out I've got another pawn?"

"Look. I don't want to be any trouble." Feeling sober, I retook control of my body and stepped forward. "If you can just pop me back in my world, I'll go to bed and forget all of this happened. I had too much to drink; this is probably a dream anyway. Right?"

The Devourer of Worlds didn't say anything. Raucous yells drew my attention beyond her. Dozens of gendered and genderless entities were milling around what looked like a conference hall. They divided their attention between screens floating in front of them and a much bigger one floating beyond them. I say hall, but there weren't any walls, or floors, or ceilings: just people and furniture standing in the emptiness of space.

They were watching a pair of armoured beast-like men fighting what looked like a goblin from the many games taking inspiration from Tolkien's creations. There were banners all over the place with symbols and scripts I didn't recognise. It looked like an international e-sports tournament where no one was playing. More curious than their strange forms were the plethora of blue boxes. There were so many, I could barely identify the details on any of them.

"I don't even want to know what's going on here. Just send me home. I'll leave all cats alone for the rest of my life. I promise."

Boots looked between the two of us and meowed once again. She trotted over to me and rubbed up against my leg.

"I understand you like him, Miss Purrfect, but you're on holiday! Why couldn't you just spend a few decades hanging out with him until you got bored or he died?" The Devourer of Worlds let out an exasperated sigh. She went from a godlike entity to very human in seconds. She couldn't stay mad at her cat the same way I always forgave Samantha's little critters for knocking my lemonade can off the coffee table. "You know what's going to happen now, right? I can't keep him here, or they'll kick me out of the game."

Boots meowed again.

"What do you mean so what?" The Devourer of Worlds hissed. "I've put everything I have into **Game World**. If they kick me out, you'll have to go back to being my herald again. Which means, you can kiss your kitten form goodbye. Do you want to go back to how things used to be?"

The meows were getting angry now.

"Look. Enough is enough." I stormed up to the woman. "You're going to tell me what the fuck is going on. Now!" I saw my reflection in her hair. Illuminated in her body's light, I was glad to see that I still looked like myself and not the monstrosities behind her. "I was just about to enjoy some cheesy chips with gravy. The potato might be soggy, but it's probably still warm. Send me back now!"

Boots hissed. Both the Devourer of Worlds and I recoiled, taking a step back.

"Fine," she said, finally acknowledging me. "Listen here, I'm putting a lot on the line for you. Alright? Just stay out of the Game."

"What Game are you talking about?" I asked as she clicked her fingers. Another blue screen popped into existence in front of me.

〖Pacifist: Combat spells and masteries growth rate reduced by 50%. Non-combat spell growth increased by 50%. Non-combat masteries growth increased by 75%〗

〖All hostile creatures are less likely to attack you unless they're starving or you slight them〗

〖Inflicting harm to any person or animal in combat will reduce all your stats by 50%. Debuff needs to be slept off〗

"Look, I'm sorry okay," she said. "The only other option is erasing you from existence. Just don't get in the way of other Champions and live your life."

I looked back at the massive screen. It displayed a burning village. A mage floating above it rained fireballs on giant insectoid monstrosities, while a militia struggled to push them back.

"You're sending me in there like this?" I asked. My heart should've been beating out of my chest right now. Did I no longer have a body? Why the hell did I have to pick up that damn cat? "Please, I just petted your cat. I wasn't going to keep her. I promise. I don't know whether this is real or not. You can't send me in there unable to defend myself. That would be murder!"

She'd gone back to ignoring me.

〖Race selection limited〗

〖Starting location set〗

"Look, can't we talk about this. If you're sending me in there, give me something to protect myself. Please. Or at least, let me go get my dinner."

I felt the weight of my guitar case on my shoulders before blinding white consumed my vision.

Chapter 2
Race Selection

My voice didn't echo in the endless white void and I didn't cast a shadow either. Then again, I probably didn't have a body. Someone must have shoved me into a half-rendered simulation. I half expected to wake up in bed with cold chips next to me.

I heard a click behind me. When I turned around, I saw a wooden door floating in the white expanse. Was I waiting for someone to come through? Or did they expect me to go through it? I couldn't tell. There was no way to track time in wherever-I-was, and my phone was no longer in my pocket. After waiting for what felt like forever, I marched up to the door and pulled it open.

"Excuse me?!" The man on the other side jumped. He was wearing a frilly shirt and a jacket out of the early eighteen hundreds, but no trousers. "I'm getting dressed here! Did they not teach you to knock in your backwards little world?"

"I'm sorry," I mumbled, feeling sheepish.

"Get out! I'll be with you in a moment." I backed away, struggling to look anywhere but at him. "Close the door!"

I did as instructed. Thinking back, it was wrong of me to assume he was a man. He had nothing between his legs, only smooth skin like a barbie doll. I had undressed and painted enough of my sister's toys to know. I wasn't being mean: she preferred her dolls have alien origins than be from boring old Malibu. She'd love it here. To be sure, I took a peak in my jeans.

Good.

Nothing was missing.

My patience was running thin. So, I was on the verge of checking on my guitar when the door finally opened. The androgynous individual came through perfectly groomed and hair slicked back. They would've looked no different from a human if not for their moonlight-silver hair and pointed ears. More importantly, there was no text box above their head. Did they not have one? Or had I lost the ability to see them?

"I wasn't expecting a new champion for quite some time," they said. It was more a complaint than an apology for keeping me waiting. "Normally, they give me enough notice to dress and prepare choice models." Getting a proper look at me, they froze. The person's shoulders drooped, and sympathy replaced the obviously annoyed expression on his face. "Ah. I see what happened. You're an anomaly. Which one of them is it this time?"

"What do you mean? There are others like me?"

"Once in a while, the Big-Cs will get overzealous and think they're about to rank up; thus preemptively finding a champion. Sometimes one of their emissaries will mess up and nab someone without checking first. Then, guess who has to clean up while the guilty parties try to hide it from one another?" They shook their head as they walked up and placed a hand on my shoulder. "Let's have a look at what they stuck you with."

A screen much like what the cosmic horrors were watching popped up an arm's length from my face.

Identification:
    First Name: —
    Race: *Unassigned*
    Health: *Error*
    Family Name: —
    Patron: —
    Mana Core: *Error*

Stats:
    Brawn: 0
    Mind: 2
    Charisma: 3
    Control: 0
    Arcana: 0
    Perception: 1

Traits:
    Pacifist

"Pacifist?!" the individual exclaimed while rolling their eyes. "That's a death sentence. You poor thing. Whoever did this to you must have really messed up."

"I know, right? She wanted to wipe me from existence instead. I swear the D—"

"Don't tell me who it was. I know I asked before, but it's best for the both of us if you keep their name to yourself. I'm Solas Frectin the Sixth: your transition agent. I'm here to help you prepare for **Game World**."

"First tell me this: what the fuck is **Game World**?" I asked, shrugging his still present hand off my shoulder. "Some sort of twisted menagerie?"

"It's a game for everyone, not on the planet. The greater cosmic entities of the Universe got bored of their basic urges and mortals aeons ago. They needed a source of entertainment for the rest of eternity, so the Originator put it together," Solas explained, shaking his head. "It's sick, I know. Instead of looking for prey or communicating with their cults, they have their emissaries look for champions on inhabited planets. Then, said champions come my way, I give them a form best suited for surviving **Game World** and send them through."

"Hold on, greater cosmic e—"

"Following that, fate is in their hands. Whenever a champion gains victory over another, their patron accumulates points. When they have enough points, the deity ranks up and can get more champions. If their champion dies, they lose points and rank down. Then there is the gambling as well. It's what makes things ruthless," they said, ignoring my interruption.

"Why do the champions play along?" For the life of me, I couldn't figure out why the champions didn't just sit tight and refuse to take part in the barbaric game. "What's stopping them from going to a pub and drinking themselves to death? Or moving to a mountain top and living their lives in seclusion?"

"Nothing. But for every champion that does so, there are ten fighting for glory," Solas spoke like they used to be one of them. They didn't volunteer the information, and more concerned for me than them, I didn't ask. "The deities bless victors with boons and riches—even powerful relics when they can afford it. Of course, there is the promise of immortality as well. Everlasting life is a real favourite when the champions find out it's a possibility. I find, in most cases, the promise of wealth and power is enough, but I digress. Let's get started with race selection. I have a roast in the oven, and my partner gets awful crabby if the meat gets dry."

Solas waved their hands and circles of darkness opened up on the floor. Different versions of myself rose up through the holes, dressed in a variety of differing garb, all with a guitar much like mine slung over their shoulders. I wasn't sure whether the aforementioned emissaries brought the creatures populating our fictions from around the cosmos, or **Game World's** designers found inspiration in mythologies and popular culture from around the Universe.

A tall, elegant version of myself looked at me down his long, thin nose. The dickhead then give me the finger. Cheeky jackass. The word 『Aelf』 appeared above his head.

"That's rude," I said, returning the gesture.

"Yeah, Aelves are like that," Solas said. "Due to their status as the most beautiful humanoids in Game World, they've developed a *major* superiority complex. Overall, Aelves aren't a bad pick. They're magically gifted and lead **Game World** in music and theatre. Being in high demand, they enjoy a fair bit of diplomatic freedom. However, deep down, nobody really likes them due to the air of pretence they give off."

I realised then that my options weren't limited to just humanoids. There were four and six-legged beasts, blobs of goo and anthropomorphic trees on display as well. Fascinating as they were, I discounted them immediately. I don't want anyone to think less of me, but, my first thought was how I'd deal with my carnal instincts. Sure, doggy-style was fun and all, but I certainly didn't want to try it out as a canine.

The choice was obvious. Or rather, I was impatient and wanted to be done with the process as soon as possible—so I marched forward and poked the aelf. On contact, an electric shock coursed through my ephemeral body, knocking me back several feet.

"Huh. They're not making it easy for you at all, are they?" Holes appeared under the aelf and several other powerful-looking versions of myself. Instead of sinking into the openings, their faces twisted into panicked expressions before falling into the darkness. "Your race selection is severely limited."

"Yeah. The bitch wants me to lay low and stay out of trouble." Only a handful of humanoids remained with different manners of herbivore-looking beasts and plump insectoids in between. "I don't fancy being a slug or rabbit, can you make anything not close to my form disappear?"

"Certainly," Solas said. Everything not standing on two legs was the next to go.

A half dozen candidates remained. A lot less than the scores if not hundreds of options I had seen before. "Can I see their stats, qualities, traits or any information that might help me decide?"

"All you need to do is touch them."

The first in line was the goblin-like creature I had seen on screen. He was short, only coming up to my waist, with green-grey skin. He looked like a starving version of myself with severe skin problems ranging from eczema to warts. His head was shaped like a pineapple laid on its side that tapered on the ends. Its pointed ears didn't help either. Unlike the aelf's, the monstrosities jutted out of the sides of its head, pointing in opposite directions like bicycle handle bars. I was hesitant to touch him but wanted a basis of comparison.

Capper:
    These cave-dwelling critters are the most misunderstood intelligent race of Game World. Sure, they might be small, ugly, and frail, but they are not to be underestimated. Naturally mischievous and tribe oriented, cappers can grow into a real threat if left to their devious and inventive ways unchecked. While their magic is ancient and ritualistic, it is surprisingly effective and can be devastating when paired with capper tinkering.

Very few gods of Game World consider cappers worthy of boons and blessings. However, the Lords of Shadows and the First Tinkerer bless them with growth bonuses in the relevant masteries.

With every achievement, boon, or blessing earned, cappers gain one attribute point for Control and Perception, and one additional statistic point to spend as they please.

"Achievements grant stats?" I asked, trying to figure out the system.

"Of course. Why else would anyone give a crap about them?" Solas rebutted. "Just so you know, for more targeted stat growths, you will need to spend time researching the different masteries. Every time you rank one up to a new milestone, you'll get a few points to distribute between the relevant stats."

"What about levelling?"

"What do you mean by that?"

"You know, grind some monsters, get experience, level up?"

"This might be a game for the Cosmics, but for you its reality. There are no stupid levels or damned respawns like the games on your backwater planets." Solas laughed. "Be thankful there is a system at all, or poor saps like you would be screwed straight out of the gate."

I discounted the capper straight away. It was likely I wouldn't survive long with the Pacifist trait crippling me. Neither did I want to live out the rest of my existence with patchy hair, scaly skin, and the rest of the package.

The hair covered entity next to him went ignored as well. As groomed and pretty as he was, I couldn't see any skin under the thick curtain of curling locks. There was no way I was going to put up with the grease and body odour that came with such a body.

The next candidate was a short walk away and a much better-looking option.

> Wood Aelph:
> Distant relatives to the Aelves, they're humble folk. Preferring nature to civilisation, they travel the fields and forests of Game World, repairing damaged ecosystems and driving away disease. Being peaceful, they abhor violence and prefer solving their problems with song and dance. As a direct result, the more powerful races have taken to capturing them to be used as songbirds. Inversely, other races adore their delightful nature and seek to protect them.
>
> Wood aelphs are loved by all deities of nature, song, and dance. They gain a bonus to all healing and plant-based magic, as well as performance-related masteries.
>
> With every achievement, boon or blessing earned, wood aelphs gain one attribute point to Arcane and Charisma, and one additional statistic point to spend as they please.

Looking at the grinning shoulder-height doppelganger, I wondered whether he was my best bet. He was as handsome as the elf while his skin had a warm earthy glow. As I circled him, his skin took on a light green hue. It wasn't a sickly green, but one that reminded me of grass after a fresh rain.

The only thing that concerned me about picking a wood aelph was the chance of ending up as someone's personal slave-jester. As much as I loved singing and playing the guitar, I didn't want to do either for table scraps. Still, it was better than the hairball and discount-goblin.

As I moved on, he shot me a cheerful grin and waved goodbye. His friendliness put a smile on my face.

Chapter 3
Armed with a Smile

The next candidate was a long walk away and turned out to be wholly unimpressive. He was the most compact of the options, vertically challenged and all that. He had a head of messy curls, pointed ears similar to the wood aelph's (but more human), all tied together with giant, hairy feet. However, the facial features weren't necessarily ugly, just out of place and certainly not in proportion to the rest of the body.

> Jovian:
> The inhabitants of Game World either love jovians or like jovians. There is no hating them. They avoid big cities, preferring instead to build their settlements on the fringes: just close enough to enjoy some measure of protection. Jovians possess the knack and passion for growing and nurturing—spending their days with their crops or livestock. They pass their evenings in the local pubs, sharing brews and singing the night away. Inversely, the rare, adventurous jovian will travel the world selling the finest mead, spirits, and tobacco. Can *you* hate them?
>
> Jovians naturally struggle with combat, tinkering and powerful magic, but nearly all deities seek to protect them. Jovians enjoy a growth bonus to all masteries not related to combat, metalworking and powerful magics.
>
> With every achievement, boon or blessing earned, jovians gain two Charisma attribute points, and one additional statistic point to spend as they please.

As ordinary as he looked, I couldn't help but like the jovian version of myself when he raised his mug at me. He seemed like a solid pick. What concerned me was his limitation with magic. I didn't know how accessible the Arcane was in **Game World,** but hoped to counter my weaknesses with defensive magic. In comparison, the wood aelph's bonus with nature and healing magic made the race a big selling point and seemed like the more balanced option.

The more I thought about it, I realised even the capper would be a better option. As tempting as picking a pub dwelling future was, cappers sounded like they had the means to protect themselves. Maybe I could put my knowledge of mathematics to use and pair it with what I remembered from A-Level Mechanics. Tinkering and sneaking about would be great for survival.

I glossed over the description of sea aelphs. They weren't too different from their terrestrial-bound cousins, but I dismissed the race without hesitation. If **Game World** had monsters like the insects that were attacking the villages, there were bound to be sea serpents, megalodon-sized sharks and other leviathans lurking about in the depths. Besides, I wasn't the strongest swimmer, and after several close calls at the deep end of the pool, I wasn't too keen on building my new life around unfathomable depths.

The final choice was a short walk away. So, I struck up a conversation with Solas.

"Which of the six do you think would serve me best?" I asked

"As a neutral party, I'm not allowed to give you such information," they answered.

"My status says I don't have a patron. That means I'm unaffiliated. Right?"

"I suppose I could tell you what I'd do in your position." They took a moment to consolidate their thoughts. "I would pick one of the less humanoid races. They work off a more evolution based system as opposed to the Masteries; certain evolutions allow you to transform or even drop traits. Or, if I decided to stick to it, certain beasts can mask their presence or become near indestructible. However, looking at your artifact, I doubt you'd be willing to go for anything of the kind."

"My artifact?" I searched my pockets, unsure of what he was referring to.

"That primitive stringed box on your back. Have you not noticed how your possible future forms all have different clothes and accessories, but the instrument is a consistent presence?"

It was.

"There are rules in **Game World**," Solas said. "Your patron may have severed all ties with you, but the rules of **Game World** demand no champion enter empty-handed."

"What about champions that don't pick a humanoid form?"

Solas didn't seem to mind my interruption. Instead, he smiled. Perhaps not all champions engaged him in conversation and made queries as I did. Whatever the case, it seemed like Solas was having a good time talking to me. "Sending someone that picks a blob of slime in with a sword would be a cruel joke."

"Not all scouted individuals come to the Cosmic Horror Gambling Association as a humanoid, and not all Cosmics are stupid," he told me. "More often than not, they can predict whether their champion will decide to go humanoid, beastial or insectoid. If it's either of the latter two, instead of an artifact, they'll receive a boon or be born with a mutation that'll give them a distinct advantage."

"Given the nature of the Pacifist trait and that artifact, you're better off picking a form that has dexterous fingers, and can get the most out of your instrument. Something with high Control and either Arcane or Charisma."

I stopped and pulled the guitar case off my back. Unzipping the semi-hard case, I retrieved my beloved instrument. If I hadn't pestered the

Devourer of Worlds, she might have stuck me with a physical boon designed for survival instead of the artefact. It may have allowed me a much better chance at survival, but I wouldn't have it any other way. I'd worked the maximum number of hours my status as a student would allow and lived off tinned tuna and lettuce for three months to save for the beauty. Nothing would take her from me, save for prying my cold, dead fingers off the fretboard.

All the possible versions of me carried similar but more aged versions of it. A historical interpretation, I suppose. If **Game World** was my future, I'd be much happier going in with a guitar than I would with the ability to breathe fire or whatever else the Cosmics granted their bestial champions.

> **Unnamed Elder Wood Guitar**
> As with any artefact, this guitar may not be lost and may be teleported to its owner once a day. Made from the fallen branch of the lost Tree of Life, it will repair itself from all damage over time.
>
> When played, it draws Mana from the atmosphere to replenish its owner's Core.
>
> It encourages weaving Mana into the music created when playing it.
>
> Charisma + 1
> Arcana + 2

On closer inspection, my guitar was more or less the same except for the crystal sphere socketed into the wood behind where the body met the neck. It was bright and empty. This changed things.

Maybe the Devourer of Worlds hadn't sentenced me to death after all. She had been fair. The guitar gave me a fighting chance. Okay. Perhaps not a *fighting* chance, but it made survival a possibility. Though, I didn't know what to expect of **Game World**, so my mind was racing with possibilities.

"Solas, can you explain what defeating a champion entails?" I asked. "I wouldn't have to kill anyone would I?"

"No. The rules are more complicated than that. Killing is by far the most straight-forward method, but defeat can come in many forms. Destroying an individual financially or politically for instance. Besting an opposing champion, at the fundamental level, simply requires you to inflict a loss of some sort that they can never recover from. The method is irrelevant in that regard, only the results matter."

"In that case, what happens to a defeated champion?"

"They lose their link to their patron," Solas answered. "Cosmics can only commune with their champions and observe the world from their perspective. The rules don't permit the Cosmics from contacting them in any other way."

Due to the Pacifist trait, I would never be as powerful as the Mage I'd seen on the big screen. Assuming the statistics did what they did in the games I'd grown up playing, Charisma was the key. With Arcana, sure I'd find some modicum of power and potential for survival, but due to my limitations, I'd always be the support figure. Maybe with Charisma, I could strike back at the Devourer of Worlds and the entities running this barbaric game. I wouldn't take down their Champions with brute force. Instead, I'd find my own way to pull ahead.

I no longer cared what the last option was. With my mind made up, I marched back towards the jovian and made my decision. He offered me his hand, and I shook it.

Then we were one.

"Interesting choice," Solas said. "Now to assign you an identity." They snapped their fingers. "Done!"

I tried summoning my status screen, but it didn't work.

"Your interface is resetting. You won't be able to view it until you're in **Game World**." Solas waved at the remaining race models, they waved back and sank into the floor. It was just us in the endless expanse of white. "All that's left to do is pick a starting location. Oh, wait," Solas changed their tune, staring at the air in front of them, probably studying a screen of their own. "You don't have a choice there. It's not a bad place to start."

"I guess, I owe you one, Solas." I offered them my hand, and they shook it. When I first arrived, we were more or less the same height, but now I barely reached their chest. "If you hadn't been so candid with me, I'd have probably rushed into a bad decision."

"Just doing my job," they replied. We stood in silence for a while, and I could tell there was something on their mind. After what felt like a forever-long handshake, they finally continued, "I've been doing this for a while, and I recognised the look on your face when you picked your race. Be careful of who you make your enemies. At least until you have enough Charisma, or Arcana, or friends to help you survive. It's not an easy world, and the more power you gain, the bigger the target on your back becomes."

I had more to say, but Solas turned on their heel and walked back to their door. They opened it and walked through. I thought Solas were about to close the door when they turned and looked at me. Solas opened their mouth as if to say something, but hesitated, unsure if they should venture to speak. Then, Solas's face hardened as they hardened their resolve.

"You picked well. Maybe with Charisma, you have a chance. The Cosmics don't play fair. In **Game World**, you'll find fallen members of their kind, gods born of the world's magic and powerful beasts. Perhaps Charisma will help you get a higher being's attention. If you can find one to become your patron, maybe you'll have a fighting chance."

Solas closed the door, and the expanse of white winked out of existence.

Chapter 4

Behind Capper Bars

Holy shit.

Maybe not holy shit. The Devourer of Worlds isn't a title a holy entity deserves. Maybe being a Cosmic Horror warrants her the new cuss: Cosmic shit. When I found out she had already locked my starting location, I expected to find myself in the boonies somewhere, not in a damned cell.

I had no idea where I was. A distant lamp served as the only source of light, and more cells lay on either side and opposite of mine. Most of the cells were empty except for the cell directly opposite mine and another two cells to the right. I saw a pointy-eared woman in the former, and there was a tall, skinny man in the latter.

I needed to get out, but one thing was for sure: I wasn't about to fight my way to freedom. Whoever imprisoned me, was strong enough to capture people twice my size. Besides, with the Pacifist trait weighing me down, I wouldn't likely get far once hit by the debuffs.

Right! I had a body now. My stats wouldn't be as pathetic as before. So with a thought, I pulled up my profile screen.

⌜ **Identification:**
    First Name: Peregrin   **Last Name:** Kanooks
    Race: Jovian   **Patron:** None
    Condition: Healthy   **Mana Core:** Empty
Stats:
    Brawn: 1   **Control:** 5
    Mind: 3   **Arcana:** 1
    Charisma: 5   **Perception:** 4

Traits:
   Pacifist
   <Unassigned>

What kind of name was Peregrin Kanooks? Was I the reject from the Fellowship of the Ring? Maybe the special half man that got sent home?

I needed to figure out the various stats. So, I tried focusing on the individual elements on the screen. Nope. This wasn't like an RPG after all. No tooltip popped up to explain my query. I'd have to figure things out on my own.

"Hey!" I shouted. "What am I in here for?"

None of my fellow prisoners so much as stirred.

I checked if I had any skills. If there was a menu with stats and traits, there had to be abilities to go with it. Much to my disappointment, I received a directionless notification.

Masteries will unlock when User has displayed sufficient proficiency in the relevant skills. If the User is already familiar in said field, Mastery will automatically rank up to an appropriate skill level.

So, no skills then.

I tried my best to piece together what the different statistics meant. I guessed Brawn was a combination of Strength and Constitution. Control had to be Dexterity and Agility, while Mind was probably Intelligence combined with Wisdom. Then again, has Wisdom ever been a real thing? What would it determine? No Mind had to be somehow related to memory and processing power. This was reality, not a video game. Surely, adding points to a screen wouldn't make me smarter or wiser.

The rest weren't so obvious. Arcana was somehow related to magic and mana. Perception obviously affected my senses while Charisma was an enigma. In every game, I've ever played, it has always been a vague concept. Higher Charisma usually meant an increase to bartering ability, access to more quests and additional information from otherwise suspicious characters. In some games, they'd make the individual more physically attractive, or have an irresistibly magnetic personality. Whatever the case, I was sure of one thing: Charisma would pair well with my relic.

I'd picked the jovian race because of its likability. From the description, it'd looked like the race would benefit the most from the stat. If you like someone, you're less likely to kill them. Right? So then, why had I been imprisoned? What had I done?

As if to answer my question, a silhouette appeared at the end of the corridor. He, she, they, whatever gender they were, pushed a cart towards us. When it got closer, I recognised the creature from the available pool of races. It was a capper. Of course. The Devourer of Worlds had put me in a dungeon run by the one goblin-like race.

The capper came down the corridor, grumbling all the while. The cart's wheels weren't coping well with the uneven stone floor.

"Wake up, ye lazy slobs," it said, sounding oddly Scottish. "Get yer tea before it gets cold. It's colcannon and black pudding night."

"I'm not eating your filthy slop," the pointy-eared woman growled. "Just put an end to it already. Kill me, eat me, do whatever you want. I refuse to spend another moment in this pigsty!"

The capper twisted a knob on his cart, and a light at its head brightened. I got a good look at the two of them. It was as I guessed, the capper was male. Despite her status as a prisoner, the woman was gorgeous. The dirt on her skin and the grime in her hair did nothing to hamper her beauty. Probably an aelf.

"Eat you? What nonsense is that?" the capper laughed. "You were caught trespassing in our land, days from the Summit. This is only a safety precaution. If yer not going to eat, that's no problem of mine." he turned around to shine his light in my cell. "What about you, half-man? Are ye on hunger strike too? Cook doesn't like it when you lot turn down food."

"I'll take it, I love colcannon." I stuck my hands through the bars, and he put a bowl in my hands. After ladling a giant dollop of mash, he topped it with black chunks of sausage. The smell was divine, and I could see the bits of fried carrot and cabbage mixed in with the mashed potato. What more could I ask for? "Thanks, mate. This looks like proper home cooking. You wouldn't happen to have any gravy on the cart, would you?"

The capper looked at me, taken aback. I guess my cheer threw him off. True, I was in a cell, but when served good food, how else would you react?

"I'm sorry, lad," he said. "Spilt it on me way down. Was a good one too. Wild boar's head and plenty of onions."

"Damn, that must have been amazing. Oh well. Still, thank your Cook for me, yeah."

"Will do, lad!" He grinned from ear to ear, his demeanour changing as we continued our conversation. On second thought, cappers weren't that ugly or backward. Was the tooltip outdated? "You know your food do, ye?"

"I do." Thinking on my feet, I came up with a quick story. "I grew up working in my uncle's tavern. Cooked the meals, scrubbed the pans, played some songs for the guests. You know how it goes."

"Boy, I do lad. There is an excellent little place near the stables, Klinkle's. If you ever get out, step in and say, hi. Best stews and brews in town."

"Now that I have you here, mister—I didn't get your name, mate."

"It's Gorin Biggut the Second, but I like ye. So, you can call me Gor." The aelf was looking at us, confused. Despite her hunger strike, Gor and I were chumming it up like old buddies. Within moments his tone had changed from rough to cheerful. It was a jarring shift, but I guess that meant I was using my Charisma just right.

"What did you need, lad? Is your cot too high for you? We mostly put big folk in here. We have a cell block for people our size, but the warden was worried them other cappers would gobble you up." Gor looked back at the aelf. "Not literally, of course. They're just a rougher crowd than what a jovian is used to."

"I appreciate that, but I wanted to discuss something else," I said, lowering my voice. Both of my fellow prisoners were focused on us now. "What am I in here for?"

"By the Shades, man. How drunk were you?"

I shrugged.

"You came to the city saying you were here to sample our local brews. We didn't think it was a big deal. Jovian merchants often stop by to sample local products." Everything sounded pretty standard so far. What did the Devourer of Worlds make me do? Rather, what did she make these cappers think I did? "Well, you got absolutely sloshed, lad. Then you whipped out your guitar and started a lovely ballad dedicated to all the girls in the crowd. What was it?"

He scratched at his big green head, trying to remember. Getting impatient, I felt tempted to rush him, but I reasoned my Charisma was helping me get through to him. The last thing I wanted to do was blow it. "That's right! You called it 'She's So Lovely'. Said it was perfect when scouting for girls. Then the capper lasses gathered round, you looked around the crowd and changed the words to 'She's So Ugly'."

Oh. That did sound like something I'd do. Maybe the Devourer of Worlds hadn't strayed far from how I got after half a dozen pints. Or did she drop me off in the pub and did I do all of that myself? I'd never know.

"Well, the shaman's daughter was out for her coming of age drink, lad. Ye pissed off a lot of people."

"Can't I make a public apology?" I asked. "As makers of good brews, you should know. You can't hold a man liable for what he does under the influence."

"On the contrary, lad, when half a barrel down, ye speak yer heart's truth. That's what we cappers say. Sit tight. We'll get to yer trial in a year or two. I'll tell Cook you like his food. We'll figure something out."

A year or two. No. Fucking. Way.

Dejected, I looked around my cell. The wooden box with a hole on top was clearly the toilet. I didn't see any toilet paper, but there was a washbasin and two cups. I imagined they practised some sort of self-bidet. The lack of soap seemed very unhygienic though. It didn't matter. I was going to get out. I didn't know how or with what, but they weren't going to keep me for long.

Next to the bars to my right, sat a cot. It was pretty high for my new size, and I cursed my measly Brawn score of one when struggling to climb onto it. I had to be missing something. Surely, the Cosmics had a rule preventing one of their ranks from dooming a prospective champion. Or did they have the freedom to do whatever they wanted to the people in their retinue?

I scanned the menus at my disposal. My guitar wasn't in the cell with me. I could summon it, but then the Cappers would likely take it away and take precautions to make sure I didn't do it again. Besides, what good would a guitar do now? Crossing my legs, I focused on my meal. Cook was talented, indeed.

Brainstorming options, I opened my status again. I hadn't paid attention to the traits the last time. 'Unassigned' drew my attention. How did I miss it before? When I focused on it, a screen appeared in front of my eyes.

> Jovians are blessed with two traits when they come of age. You have one and may pick another.
>
> You may choose from the following three options:
>
> Nimble Hands:
> Your natural Control and race have made your fingers agile and dexterous. Whether you're picking locks or pockets, weaving cloth or playing an instrument, nimble hands are your friends. Your base Control is twice as effective when your hands are involved.
>
> Finders Keepers:
> Closer to the ground, you're more likely to spot anything shiny and useful. You may activate the trait to discover something that may help you out of a predicament. Gain an additional charge for every ten Perception. Charges replenish after a full night of sleep.
>
> Blinding Charisma:
> A winning smile is useless if people can see right through you. Sometimes, a distracting smile or an intimidating aura needs a little bit of help. 25% more Perception is needed to resist effects born of Charisma.

This wasn't going to be an easy choice. I didn't know what enabled me to pick a trait, and when I'd get the chance to pick again, but they all looked handy. Curious, the perks were very specific to my current situation. It was as if the system was wary of what I needed. Maybe the Cosmics didn't have full control over it, and the system was designed to give everyone a chance at survival and success.

Finders Keepers looked like the best option, but I wasn't sure. I didn't intend to invest in Perception. Still uncertain on how the system worked, I wasn't sure whether I would have the points to spare. So, I discounted it as an option.

At first, Blinding Charisma looked like a brilliant candidate, but I didn't know how stats scaled for everybody else and how much Charisma I'd need before getting use out of it, so I avoided picking it as an option.

Nimble Hands was the opposite. In the long term, I could see it becoming a vital perk for my growth, but it wouldn't help me get out of prison. Even if I knew how to pickpockets, Gor didn't come close to the bars, and I doubted he had the keys on his person. Still, it felt like a better option.

"I wouldn't do that if I were you," a voice said, making me jump.

Chapter 5
Baby don't lie no more

Sitting up, I looked at my fellow prisoners. I heard snoring from the man, while the aelf woman lay on her cot, looking away from me. It wasn't either of the two, I was sure. It was too early for me to lose my sanity: barely an hour had passed of my existence as a conscious prisoner.

I went to select the perk again.

"Seriously, that's a bad choice," it said again.

"Who's there?" I whispered, worried that I might actually be going insane. "Please be real."

"You're not crazy," the voice laughed. "Look up."

There was nothing on the ceiling. No hole, grate or any other opening for someone to talk through. All I saw was the same rocky surface that constituted the walls. It looked like the cappers had only bothered carving out the floor and raising the ceiling where required. Even then, it was only high enough for someone of capper or my stature to traverse quickly. Full-sized folk like the aelf woman would probably have to crouch to get through.

I lay back down and focused on the screen. Was it my conscious trying to stop me? I was reaching for my selection again when a fingernail-sized spider rappelled through the screen.

"Do you see me now?"

A shrill, lady-like scream escaped my lips as I smacked the little bug away.

"Hey! That's not nice!" the voice exclaimed. "I just want to talk."

"Spiders don't talk!" I hissed. I didn't want my neighbours to think I was crazy. "You don't have the brain capacity for speech, let alone vocal cords."

"I didn't think you were so small-minded."

Was it making a joke? Whoever heard of a spider making a joke? I really was going insane. Then it was there again. My attack hadn't dislodged the spider from its silken stand. Now, it was swinging back and forth through my screen.

"Look, if you'll just listen, I'm here to help."

"Do a lot of people accept help from talking spiders?" I asked. I let the screen remain where it was. With its blue glow as a backdrop, I could see the spider easily.

"No, but you'd think in a world where gods walk amongst men, Cosmic powers are a proven entity and monsters don't just inhabit myths and fairy tales, people would be more open-minded," the voice answered. "I'm merely using this spider form as a conduit. A friend called in a favour, so I thought I'd offer you some help."

"Why would anyone want you to help me? I don't know anyone here."

I jumped into an upright position on hearing a soft meow next to my ear. It was Boots. As soon as I was upright, she jumped into my lap. She was a lot bigger than I remembered her. No. Boots was the same size. I was just smaller.

"No, I'm not saying that, Miss Purrfect," the spider said.

Boots meowed again.

"Fine. Miss Purrfect says you do her scritches just right. She wants to help, so that you'll be in a better mood when she visits for future sessions."

Oh. She was the antagonist here. Boots caused all of this. However, looking at the cat and realising she'd brought a friend to help, I couldn't stay mad at her. Or, was this some mind trick she had brewing? As much as I loved cats, trusting one felt like a bad idea. Oh well. Nothing I could do about it now. So, I scratched the top of her head, and Boots' ears went flat. She closed her eyes and purred.

"Who're you?" I asked.

"I go by many names, but you may call me Maka."

"Fine then, Maka, which perk would you recommend? They both look pretty useful to me."

"They're all good," Maka replied. "Just not what you need right now."

"I know I'm new to this world and the rules are probably different. But where I come from, you don't accept gifts from disembodied entities or make deals with someone or something you don't know. It *never* ends well in the stories."

"Well, it's a good thing I'm not asking you to make a deal," the spider said. "I'm repaying a favour. That's all."

Boots swatted my hand away. She rested a paw on either shoulder and stood in my lap. Looking into my eyes, she meowed.

"Fine."

Facts Begin With Fiction:
Your songs and stories soften the crowd. If your Charisma is sufficient, targets become more open to your truths and lies. Beings with high Perception may see through your attempts, but that won't necessarily affect their willingness to accept your songs and stories.

"What good will that do me?" I was starting to get annoyed now. Sure, getting to pet a cat made me feel better, and I appreciated she was trying to help, but storytelling wouldn't get me out of my current predicament. "I don't like spiders. So, if you'll just go away, I'd like to find my own way out."

"What's there not to like about spiders?!" Maka exclaimed, sounding shrill, like an excitable little girl. "You befriend one spider. Eventually, you'll befriend us all. We are everywhere and *very* helpful. With eight eyes, we see more than anyone. We spiders are hunters, trappers, scholars, and dancers. Our lifelong dream is to become storytellers, but no one wants to read the webs we weave. Become a spider's friend and accept my storytelling gift."

Boots meowed at me again. This was insane. I really was going mad. Maybe a lifetime of atheism had been a bad idea. I'd died and gone to hell, and this was my punishment. My list of sins wasn't short:

1. Premarital sex.
2. Eating more than I should.
3. Envying others for having more sex than me
4. Indulgence in the brew.
5. Regularly cursing pharmaceutical companies for not making male contraception as convenient as the pill or IUDs.

The list went on and on. This ordeal was my penance.

"Look. I'm in no position to convince anyone to listen to me, let alone sit through a whole story. I'll make this easy for you," Maka continued. "You accept the perk, and I'll rally the boys and girls. We'll ensure you get your chance to tell your story and get out of this cell..."

"Fine, if you agree to help me until I'm safe and out of the city, I'll take your word for it."

"Very well." The spider sounded annoyed. I don't know what favour or debt it owed Boots, but I was taking advantage of it. Maka didn't owe me anything, but Boots and the Devourer of Worlds certainly did.

Hoping I wouldn't regret it, I accepted the perk. It worked with Charisma as well. Hopefully, I'd get the opportunity to pick the other perks later.

📜 Congratulations!
You've befriended a divine being!
Achievement unlocked:
Friends in High Places
    Charisma + 2
You have one unassigned stat point. 📜

I added the extra point to Charisma as well. Given how freely Gor had spoken to me, I was keen to find out how far the stat would get me. I didn't trust Maka. More so because it didn't call me out for keeping its offer open-ended. I didn't intend to leave the city straight away given my Pacifist trait and my ignorance of local geography. Leaving town wasn't a particularly good idea. Hopefully, Charisma would help me avoid the law and find a secure way out.

"So, what happens now?" I asked, only to realise, Maka was gone. Boots meowed at me again. "You've got some interesting friends? That wasn't a Cosmic like your bitch of a master, was it?"

Boots looked at me angrily and swatted me with her paw. I got the message: "Don't insult the Devourer of Worlds". I wondered whether she'd be mad if I ever moved against the Cosmic entity.

There was a chill in the dungeon. I could feel the cold radiating off the stone walls. Were we high up, or was it winter in the capper corner of the world? I wondered if Gor would be willing to get me a blanket. Probably sensing my discomfort, Boots snuggled into my neck. I welcomed her warmth. When offered a chunk of black pudding, she sniffed at it before turning her head away. I was about to put it in my mouth when she grabbed my hand between her two front paws and pulled the food into her's.

I couldn't help but wonder what Boots looked like before the Devourer of Worlds put her in a cat body, but she indeed behaved like a cat. I wonder what their criteria was for picking champions. If Boots only picked individuals that petted her right, were all of the Devourer of World's champions crazy cat ladies?

The feline's body heat and soft fur lulled me into a comfortable sleep. I dreamt of the forgotten cheesy chips with gravy. It started with me enjoying the meal on my own, then, Louis came in with a giant dog head and tried to steal most of it.

Then, a sharp poke to the side woke me up. It was Gor and another capper shining a bright light in my eyes. Boots was gone, and my teeth were chattering noisily. When I sat up on the cot, my breath misted in front of my face.

"We've had a t-t-talk, and petitioned the s-s-shaman," the second capper said with a nervous stutter. "We're letting you out of your cell."

"What? Just like that?" I was surprised, to say the least. What did Maka do? Both Gor and his plus one looked more pale and sickly than their green-grey skin normally was. "Great, if we can just get Boots and my guitar, I'll be out of your hair."

"Boots?" Gor and his companion looked at one another, confused. "Ye didn't have any boots on when you got here lad. Didn't think yer lot wore any."

That's right. I was some kind of hobbit creature. I didn't need boots. In fact, my feet were the only part of my body that weren't freezing.

"Besides, you're not free to go," the other capper said. He didn't sound Scottish like Gor, just Northern. Lots of planets have a North, I suppose. "We had a word with the chief and the shaman. You're sentenced to servitude. Due to a recent mishap, Cook lost his assistant."

"What kind of mishap?" I asked.

The two cappers looked at each other with sorrowful expressions. "The lad was helping Warden, here, with some boxes and found a spider's nest. They got attacked."

Gor placed a hand on his friend's shoulder.

"I g-g-got away, but the boy fell down the stairs and b-b-broke his neck," Warden explained.

Cosmic shit. Did I just ally myself with a stone-cold killer, or was it all an accident? Sure, this wasn't the same as getting me out of the city, but it was a start. Maybe while working in the kitchens, I could put **Facts Begin With Fiction** to work.

"C'mon then, Cook should be starting for the day soon," Gor said. "We'll show you the kitchens and where you'll be sleeping."

When I got off the cot, my empty food bowl noisily clattered to the cell floor, making both of the cappers jump. Huh. It was empty. The portion which had been too big for my now small body was all but gone. Boots must have eaten it before leaving.

The male prisoner was still snoring, while the female sat up in her cot to watch me. She walked up to the bars when we left my cell. "You're not crazy then," she said. I looked at her quizzically. "I was sure you were mad when you started talking to your screens. Well, you've got to be a little insane to insult a green-skin Shaman's daughter."

Both the warden and Gor hissed at her. I guess they didn't like the term green-skin. It must be a derogatory phrase of some sort, so I hurriedly committed it to memory.

"Get them to release me too," she continued. "I promise I'll make it worth your time."

In the warden's light, I got a good look at her. Not only did she have a gorgeous face, but the rest of her was a sight to behold too. Whatever she was offering, I'd happily accept, but at the same time, receiving such offers felt rather dirty. However, when she looked into my eyes, I found myself struggling to turn her down.

"Y-Y-You're not only a suspected spy, but also the c-c-chief's prisoner," Warden stuttered. "He'll have my-y-y head if I let you go."

The aelf woman ignored him. Her eyes were still focused on mine. "If your friend is strong enough to get you out, I'm sure you can have him help me too."—Her voice was soft and sweet nectar to my ears, and her body swaying with serpentine grace as she followed me along the bars left me enamoured—"I have powerful friends too, you know. Helping me would benefit you in more than one way."

I don't think I would have ever moved from the spot if Gor didn't drag me away. "She's charming ye," he hissed. "Don't fall for it! When we found the lass, she had a warband of elite cappers feeding her grapes and massaging her shoulders."

"Why isn't she affecting you then?" I asked.

Gor held up a locket. It looked like some knucklebones and claws held together with pieces of twine. "The chief lent it to me. It's an expensive charm, but as long as her Charisma doesn't surpass thirty-five, she can't do the same to us. So long as I have this on, only an Adept or higher Mind Mage is getting in this noggin."

He was right. As soon as we turned the corner, whatever power she had exerted on me faded and I regained full mental clarity. Was this the power of Charisma, or had she cast a spell of some sort? Whatever it was, it was frightening, and I wanted to learn more.

"I pledge a life debt on the condition you help me escape!" her yell echoed down the corridors, and I felt a tug deep inside me. Thanks to the distance between us, I resisted whatever magic she was using.

I let Gor and Warden guide me up the stairs and out of the dungeons wondering if I should ask Maka to help her or not. The aelf woman's knowledge *could* come in handy.

Chapter 6
Onions Potatoes and a Whole Lot More

Despite my Charisma stat, Cook didn't like me from the get-go. I don't know whether he had too much Perception or if grumpy was his default state, but I wasn't going to ask. He took one look at me, grunted, and pointed to a sack of onions.

"What do you need, Cook?" I asked. "Roughly chopped, sliced, julienne, brunoise?"

In response, Cook sliced the sack open with a knife, took an onion and smashed it on the table with his fist. The impact crushed the vegetable, and he pulled the skin off in one piece. The onion went in a stockpot before he grunted and went back to portioning chunks of meat.

I lacked the Brawn to do the same.

⌈ **Identification:**
    First Name: Peregrin   **Last Name:** Kanooks
    Race: Jovian   **Patron:** None
    Condition: Healthy   **Mana Core:** Empty
Stats:
    Brawn: 1   **Control:** 5
    Mind: 3   **Arcana:** 1
    Charisma: 8   **Perception:** 4
Traits:
    Pacifist
    Fact Begins with Fiction ⌋

To take advantage of my new trait, I had put the extra stat point into Charisma. I just needed the opportunity to put my Fact Begins with Fiction trait to good use.

Cook kept the kitchen nice and clean, but lacked organisation. I looked around for a meat mallet or rolling pin; rummaging through a few drawers, several tubs, and even climbing onto the counter to check the top shelves. No luck. At least it got Cook to talk to me.

The tubby, middle-aged capper, banged his hand on the counter and shouted, "Use a knife for the spirits' sake!"

He pulled a chef's knife out of a wooden block and stuck it point-side down on the table. The wood easily gave way to his sheer force, and the knife handle vibrated ever slightly. Cook glared at me with his large, bloodshot eyes before returning to his workstation. I couldn't tell whether he had a problem with me, or if there was something else going on.

The chef's knife felt familiar in my hand. A wave of sorrow crashed down on me as it confirmed the truth: this was my new reality. I'd miss my dickhead of a flatmate, Louis. Mum and dad, Piya—my baby sister. Bloody hell, the thought of never seeing Samantha again and getting some closure saddened me too. Worst of all, I'd never have cheesy chips with gravy again.

Hold on a second. Did **Game World** have the same delicacy? I didn't see a deep-fat fryer in the kitchen. I imagined only the affluent could afford to splurge on litres of oil on a whim. *Maybe*, the denizens of **Game World** hadn't discovered chips or french fries yet. I had the necessary cooking skills, and Control was among my higher stats. Perhaps I could bring my favourite dishes from Earth to **Game World**! I bet the concept of a twice-baked potato would amaze the cappers.

Enthused by the possibility of fame and fortune, I peeled and chopped onions with renewed vigour.

"You're the new assistant, eh?" a capper sporting only grey trousers asked. Similar to the warden, he sounded Northern and not Scottish-Midland accent, I think. I hadn't heard him approach me or enter the kitchen. Good thing I had put the knife down for a moment, or I would've cut myself. I need a lot more than four Perception. Perhaps I'd invest in the stat once I got my Charisma to a decent level. "Good. There's no way Cook is going to feed the entire prison on his own."

"That's right, he lost his assistant, and I just so happen to prefer anything over that bloody cold cell."

The tubby capper could probably hear us, but unlike me, he didn't let himself get distracted. It explained the grumpiness. Hopefully, I'd warm up to him over time.

"You've got his knife right there." I hadn't spared the tool a second look. It had Rungo carved into the handle, and though scratched the blade had a beautifully honed edge. The knife's previous owner had taken good care of it. I should've known better than to trust a spider. "He was a good kid. It's a shame; his family won't be letting any of us attend the funeral. They're blaming us for his death. I'm Hruk by the way."

"I'm Perry. And you're the janitor?" I asked, noticing the mop and bucket behind him.

"I'm an inmate, like you," he answered. "The warden likes using non-violent criminals for free labour. There's a few of us around,"—Cook cleared his throat, making the capper flinch. Okay. Maybe he wasn't just grieving. The angry chef vibe I was getting off Cook wasn't only in my head—"I better get back to work before the onions make us cry. I don't know how Cook does it. Exposing a capper to raw onion fumes is downright cruel."

Once again, I found myself alone with a sack of onions, a knife and a stockpot. Not long after, Cook left the room grumbling and wiping at his eyes. Strange. On Earth, I would've started crying by the fourth onion. However, half a sack in and my eyes were bone dry. Was this some sort of jovian resistance? They're tiny, have giant, hairy feet, everybody likes them and possess immunity to onions. The system should've put that in the tooltip; I would've picked the race straight away. Bloody hell! I hoped the residents of **Game World** would understand my sarcasm. As a British citizen, passive-aggressive behaviour and sarcasm came naturally to me. On second thought, to put my Charisma to good use, I'd probably have to leave that part of me behind.

I emptied the sack and Cook still hadn't returned. My stomach was rumbling, and I needed something to eat. Unfortunately, I didn't know which ingredients I was permitted to use. So, I went over to the stack of sacks piled up in the corner of the room, and dug out three large potatoes. They were almost as big as my face. After poking them all over with the knife, I threw them in the wood oven. There wasn't a thermometer or a timer at hand, so I'd have to rely on my years of part-time cooking experience to judge the doneness.

The prospect of a baked potato had me salivating. So, I took the opportunity to look around the kitchen. Good. I found salt and butter. Hunting through the cupboard, I also found what I wanted: dried garlic and a coarse red spice that smelled like Sichuan pepper. Hoping Cook would take his sweet time, I put the ingredients in a pan on the stove and got cooking.

First, I browned the onions in a large knob of butter, then added the garlic to it and finished it off with the seasoning. Then came the long wait of cooking potatoes. My heart began to race; worried Cook would come back any moment. I didn't know whether this counted as stealing or not. I was just so damn hungry.

To keep myself busy, I tried organising the kitchen. However, due to the lack of space, I didn't know where to put anything. Cook had one corner dedicated to utensils and cutlery, and another to pots and pans. In between sat a sink so broad and deep, my jovian body could go swimming in it. Shelves lined the adjacent walls, and the stove stood against the fourth.

A pop from within the wood-burning oven put an end to my exploration. The potatoes were finally ready. If I weren't so impatient, I'd give them a few minutes to cool, but I attacked them as soon as they were out. I sliced the potatoes in half, lengthways, then scooped the flesh out and threw it in the pan of onions, garlic, and browned butter. I mixed and mashed the starchy goodness before piling the mixture back within the skins. After five more minutes in the oven, my meal was ready.

"In the spirits' name, what are ye doing, lad?" Just my luck. Cook had to come back just as I picked up my fork. "I left ye for—" he looked around, "how long has it been?"

"Considering how long it takes potatoes to cook, more than an hour since you left," I answered. "I'm sorry, Cook. I got hungry after finishing the onions. I didn't know how long you'd be, so I made myself some food."

The capper sighed, shaking his head. "That smells like my dried garlic," Cook said. "Ye went through my cupboard." I failed to maintain contact with his red eyes. Damn it. Why did I give in to my stomach? I had better self control on Earth. "I should've expected as much of a jovian. Yer lot think with their stomachs don't they?"

"Don't send me back the cell, Cook. I'll do better."

Instead of saying anything more, the capper took the fork out of my hands and sampled the steaming plate of savouriness.

"What do you call this?" he asked.

"Twice-baked potato."

"It's missing something."

"Cheese?" I asked.

"That's it!" Cook grinned. He dug a giant hunk of hard cheese out of his cupboard and sliced pieces of it onto the potato and ate another forkful. "I hate to admit it, lad, but maybe you're the kitchen assistant I always needed."

He clapped my shoulder and pushed one of the potatoes my way. Cutting off a bit, I tried it. The red spice had added a unique flavour I'd never tasted before.

> Congratulations! You braved getting shanked in a capper prison and brought something new to Game World! Cooking Mastery unlocked.
> For creating something spectacular, you've gained a growth bonus beyond your natural skill level.
> Cooking Mastery has progressed to Apprentice: Rank 5
>   Control + 1
>   Perception + 2

No achievement? Surely creating a new dish had to be worth a little bit more. Still, I got a boost to the stats I needed. Maybe this new life wouldn't completely suck after all.

"That's just what I needed," Cook said. "Tell me your name again, lad."

"It's Perry,"—I put on my best smile—"my mum owned a tavern," I told him. "I'm just at the Apprentice rank, but tell me what you need, and I'll get it done."

Cook's expression went placid. "You stay away from my spice cupboard, you hear me?" The change in tone took me by surprise. "I don't care what you know, this is my kitchen, and you're a convict. Step out of line again, and I'll send you back to your cell."

Chapter 7
All Hail the Chief

The twice-baked potato opened up dialogue with Cook, but he would only allow shorter conversations. So, I still didn't get a chance to take **Facts Begin With Fiction** out for a test drive. I probably had enough Charisma for the likes of Gor but not Cook. When I gave the system some thought it made sense. The capper racial bonus included Perception and Cooking Mastery added to the stat as well.

Three days passed of me working in the kitchens, but I didn't make any progress with Cooking Mastery or with Cook himself. I guessed once in the Apprentice ranks, chopping onions, peeling potatoes, and dicing carrots didn't count for much. Neither did handling hot potatoes and refilling the skins with mash. Despite how much he enjoyed the twice-baked potato, he wouldn't let me do any real cooking.

Instead, the capper had me teach him the details of my creation and made it himself for the prison staff. Once he learned the second cook gave the potato, it's texture. He adapted the dish to cater to his people's palettes. Gor and Warden both loved the dish. Cook took credit for it, but they both shot me a knowing look. Okay. Perhaps bringing Earth dishes to **Game World** would have to wait until after I got out of prison. I worried refuting my supervisor's claims would get me sent back to my cell.

The facade lasted until a new authority figure appeared. On the third day of me working in the kitchens, the Capper Chieftain, Grog, came around for inspection.

"You're stretching yourself too thin," Grog said, walking into the kitchens with Gor and Warden hot on his tail. "I'll talk to the shaman about getting more Mind Warding totems made. I don't want you working seven days a week, Gor. You'll kill yourself."

"Our people just don't know how to deal with her," Gor replied. "With or without a totem, the lass be charming."

"I know she's a beauty, but don't go falling for her," Grog joked, nudging Gor with his elbow. "Coming from a man that married outside his species, believe me, you're better off with a capper lass. Much as I love my wife, after years of dealing with the Shaman and her family, I've wondered if we'd have been better off not meeting."

Both Gor and Warden went silent at the awkward revelation. Grog turned his attention to me. With Cook busy handling raw meat, I was responsible for taking the twice-baked potatoes out of the oven. It wasn't much, but I was glad to have something to do besides working with raw vegetables.

"This must be the jovian cook I've heard so much about." The chieftain wandered over and snatched a cooked potato off the tray. "Good on you for taking the shaman's family down a notch. Was a stupid thing you did, but funny all the same." He took a bite out of the potato, and his eyes widened. "What in the Spirit's name is this?"

"A jovian delicacy, Chief," Gor said before Cook could get his answer in. The tubby capper's face reddened. "The lad brought a bit of home to Blacknail's Table."

Gor standing up for me all of a sudden took me by surprise. Did the residents of **Game World** believe in respecting intellectual property? On second thought, perhaps the concept was too advanced for my reality. Maybe he and Cook simply didn't have the best of working relationships. Whatever it was, the capper had my respect.

Up close, I clearly saw the differences between Grog and his subjects. Not only did he stand taller and had the musculature of a bodybuilder, but he also had much clearer skin. Unlike the other cappers, he didn't have any warty growths or patches of reptilian scales. Our skin only differed in complexion, and he wore his orange hair in a large mane-like fashion.

"It's a shame Rungo passed, but you've finally got an assistant that can help you achieve greatness, Cook!" Grog turned to Gor. "I appreciate everything you do for this city and facility, but I want you to take two days off a week." The chieftain clapped a massive hand on my shoulder, making me wince. "I've got your solution right here. On your days off, the jovian will make the rounds."

Gor tried to protest the issue, but Grog ignored them. They moved on, leaving Cook to explode on me. Much to my surprise, he didn't. Instead, the capper untied my apron and took it off me.

"Get out."

"I didn't say anything, Cook," I said. "Don't send me back to the cells."

"How petty do you think I am?" He frowned. "Chief will tear me a new one if he finds out that I'm making prisoners work without a break. You're off for the evening."

"What am I supposed to do? I don't have any money. Aren't you afraid I'll run away?"

"I don't care," he said. "There is only one jovian in the city and it's you. Good luck going unnoticed and getting past the gate. Even if the spirits of good fortune shine their light on you, luck can only get you so far in the wilderness beyond."

Despite his tone, Cook smiled at me. Maybe he was more than an angry old fart after all. I didn't think they'd really let me roam freely. Perhaps this was my chance to get out, maybe put **Facts Begin With Fiction** to good use. Only, exiting the city wouldn't be enough: I'd need transport to somewhere safe.

"Maka?" I whispered at the shadows outside the kitchen, "I think this might be our chance to escape."

No response. The extra points in Perception didn't help me see the details in the darker corners as I'd hoped. Didn't matter, there had to be a spider somewhere in the darkness. Either Maka couldn't hear me, or they'd chosen to ignore me. Did it lie to me? I should've known better than to put my trust in a damned spider. Its deal with Boots probably ended at getting me out of the damned cell.

"Maka?" I tried, once more.

I waited a couple of minutes before giving up hope. Not willing to waste Cook's gift, I worked my way towards the exit. The low security in the dungeons surprised me. I only saw a handful of guards, and like Hruk and I, quite a few prisoners, were working around the prison. Only I had a shirt: they all wore grey trousers and occasionally a vest. Though their feet were much smaller than mine, they had no boots on. I recalled seeing some manner of footwear on all the free cappers.

It all made sense when I exited the building. If not for my desperation to figure out an escape plan, I'd head back into the building. I had on a ripe-smelling, off-white shirt, trousers, and a pair of suspenders; no jacket, cape, or any winter wear. Passing cappers looked at me confused or worried, most likely thinking I'd gone mad. Snow as high as my thick ankles blanketed the ground.

Then it occurred to me: Cook didn't intend this as a break or reward. The tubby capper intended to punish, perhaps even kill me. Of course. Then he could claim the glory of the twice-baked potato for himself. Screw him. The system had recognised it as my invention. The world probably lacked patents, but if it did, I'd ensure everyone knew who made **Game World**'s first twice-baked potato. I planned on making it big in **Game World**. Music and potatoes. What more did a man need for fame?

Unfortunately, that would have to wait. It made sense why Cook made such warm and hearty food. The cappers likely relied on the stodginess of mashed potato and the warmth of black pudding to survive the harsh temperature. Fortunately, I wasn't starving, just at risk of freezing to death.

It looked like dusk was approaching, and the streets were just starting to fill up. Were cappers nocturnal? In the dungeons, there had been no way of telling time and given my well-rested brain, several hours had passed since my attempted conversation with Maka. Either way, with people around, maybe I would find some shelter or warmth.

The majority of the people I saw around me were cappers. Among them, I spotted a few humans and the odd, hairy individuals from race selection. Most curious of the lot was the ugly grey-skinned man pushing an empty cart.

When our eyes met, he grinned, and it gave me the creeps. I don't know whether it was his six-inch-long, hooked nose or the jagged, pointed teeth. Whatever it was, looking eye-to-eye with him, I felt like a deer staring down a bear. He reminded me of the bridge trolls out of old fairy tales, only shorter and uglier. Then, he lost interest in me and moved on, pushing his rickety wooden cart.

The prison stood behind me, built into a massive cliff wall. The rest of the city looked like a tribal settlement of titanic proportions. Only a handful of buildings were taller than two storeys. Made of stacked flat rocks and hastily nailed together pieces of wood, they looked like major safety hazards. Any city official on Earth—at least where I grew up, would slap a condemned sticker on the door and call for bulldozers to have them knocked down. And maybe even give a hefty fine for good measure at that.

The tents had sloping and rounded roofs to keep snow from collecting on top, and were arranged around communal fire pits. While wandering away from the prison, I encountered a roaring flame with only an older capper male sitting in front of it. After a little hesitation, I invited myself to his circle of warmth.

Chapter 8

Conjuror of Cheap Tricks

The capper raised an eyebrow at me, but he didn't say anything when I took a seat. He shuffled away until we were on almost opposite sides of the fire. I didn't think negatively of him. After all, I was a stranger not dressed for the weather. Looking at me, he probably thought I was either crazy or a vagrant. The fire's warmth felt pleasant on my skin. I held out my hands, letting the heat do its job.

"What're you doing here, jovian?" A young capper woman was standing behind my new aged friend, now. Distracted by the heat, I didn't see which tent she came out of. "This isn't a public fire."

"I'm sorry, miss," I said, trying my best to keep my teeth from chattering. "My warm clothes got stolen while I was napping. Do you mind if I stick around a bit to warm my bones? I promise I won't be a bother."

"I do. It's breakfast time, and Gram doesn't like guests during meals. You should be on your way."

The older capper, probably Gram, jabbered at me but I didn't understand a word. I already struggled with Scottish accents, and his lack of teeth didn't help the situation. At least they didn't guess my status as a convict straight away. Now that I thought about it, besides me, all the prisoners wore grey clothing. Perhaps it not only gave them away but also acted as a deterrent. No one in their right mind would want to escape into a frigid environment unprepared.

"That's right," the she-Capper continued, "the shaman has invited Gram for the morning spirit songs, and he wants to see the magicks. We don't want a stranger making us late."

I needed to change their minds. If all cappers were standoffish like them, I'd die of the cold. People were supposed to love jovians, but I didn't feel loved. Maybe 'loved' ended at not being put down for trespassing. I needed the chance to put **Fact Begins With Fiction** to use, but they wouldn't listen to what I had to say. Then, an idea struck.

"What if I showed you some magicks, then would you let me stay by your fire?"

Gram started speaking again, and like before, it all sounded like gibberish. When he finished the younger capper glared at me with her hands on her hips.

"I understood none of that."

She rolled her eyes at me and sighed. "You've got to start wearing your dentures Gram."

Gram's reply was short and terse.

"I don't care if the wood is uncomfortable," she said. "I'm getting sick of being your translator. I have better things to do with my life, ye know." The younger capper turned to me more irritated than before. "If you're a shaman or Mage, or whatever your people's version of a caster is, why don't you magick yourself a fire and feck off, Gram says"

Gram egged her on. He had clearly said a lot more than that.

"You're as far from a Mage as he is from aelf maiden. Gram is sure you're going to pull some stupid trick and then demand the use of our fire. We don't like squatters in this neighbourhood."

"What if I prove him wrong, though?" I asked

Gram said a handful of words and broke out into laughter.

"Nothing you do will convince him to let you stick around. However, if you can pull something magical out of that plump jovian arse of yours, we'll give you a jumper and a cloak if it'll get you out of our hair."

I couldn't ask for a better deal. Gram looked convinced that he had called my bluff. The female didn't look so sure. They weren't wrong. I didn't know any magic. Still, I had one trick up my sleeve, and I prayed to whatever entity reigned over the system, that it did not fail me now.

Summon guitar, I thought. It didn't work. Great. Maybe I should have given this some thought first. I called forth my screens and flicked through them; the tooltip didn't offer any help.

"Well?" She didn't look particularly patient.

I tried it again to no avail. Perhaps the phrasing was off? *Accio guitar*. I thought, yet nothing happened. *Abracadab-guitar*? Nope, nada.

Okay. I needed to figure this out as soon as possible. Closing my eyes, I held my left hand out, picturing my old guitar. I recalled the feeling of the smooth fretboard against my palm. Barely half a week had passed since my fingers last danced across the strings, and I still felt the familiar vibrations against my skin. Most might think it silly, but I'd named the instrument after my late grandmother, Diya. My former body had the word tattooed on its right bicep in Sanskrit and 'brown sugar' on the left one—on account of my skin colour and inherent sweetness. I wanted Diya: I missed her.

It worked! A familiar weight appeared in my hands, and Diya felt no different from when I last held her. I opened my eyes and was pleased. It was indeed my old guitar. The strings looked a lot newer than the ones I prefered; they felt softer, as well. Probably for the best. My uncalloused fingers would likely be thankful for them.

Both Gram and the female capper were staring at me, their jaws hanging open.

> You have named your relic: Diya.
> By granting it a name, you have linked the relic to your Core. It will passively feed on your Mana, but in turn, will grow at a swifter rate.

"What manner of magick was that?" she asked. "It was neither Creation nor Shaping, that much I'm sure of."

I had no idea how the magic system of **Game World** worked. I guessed those were two of however many Schools of Magic. I didn't want to give away my ignorance, so I flashed a cocky smile and hoped they didn't demand a response. My mind was drawing a blank. Fortunately, Gram didn't give me the time to answer. He fished a wooden pair of dentures out of his pockets and stuffed them in his mouth.

"I ain't too proud to admit when I've been had, laddie," he said. Gram's speech was still a challenge to decipher. He sounded more Scottish than Gor but even better than before. He pushed himself upright and shuffled towards the largest of the tents. "C'mon then, let's see what fits ye."

"Gram, you can't invite a stranger in!"

"Hush now, Klinkle. I'm four times your age. Don't tell me what I can and can't do."

I hurried after Gram before Klinkle could change his mind. Walking into the tent, I expected several rugs and cushions with sparse furniture. Instead, I found cuts of meat and fresh game hanging from hooks. For a moment I was worried the cappers had played an elaborate trick on me and were going to butcher me for dinner, but Gram walked past the drying racks and into a hole carved into the floor.

Following him felt like a bad idea. But then again, unless Gram had several cappers waiting to jump me, I would have no trouble outrunning him. As for Klinkle, I'd have to risk Pacifist's debuffs. To keep my hands free, I slung the guitar over my shoulder. It was a good thing I never removed the original's ugly, patchy-brown strap.

Much to my relief, there was no one waiting for me. I found a collection of unfinished rooms decorated with crooked wooden and metal furniture. So, most of the tents above were probably entrances for similar structures. Even though the tooltip had claimed cappers were inventive, they didn't seem particularly skilled at carpentry, metallurgy, or masonry. How did they tinker?

"Ye look like me nephew's size. Try these on." He threw a bundle of rough, woollen jumpers at me. Gram probably didn't have the best eyesight. The jumble of clothing included cardigans, jumpers and vests of varying sizes. "Don't have too many capes or coats to spare, lad. I guess you'll have to make do with one o' mine. Me kids won't let me travel anymore anyway."

Gram's hand-me-down cape proved to be a real prize. The base cloth was a faded, dark green, but an assortment of colourful and patterned patches constituted the bulk of it. It was so ugly I loved it. Trying it on, I knew it was a winner. It had a hood, a few clasps to secure it around my collarbone and bindings to tighten it around my neck as well. The length was perfect, cutting off halfway down my shins. The best part of it had to be the lengths of cloth stitched into the insides at stomach height.

"Useful, ain't they?" Gram asked while I investigated them. "Me Crivy—the spirits bless her soul—stitched them sleeves in after I lost me sixth pair o' gloves. Lets you get all nice and snug."

"Are you sure I can have this?" If I weren't as good as a pauper, I would've said no straight away. Parting an older man from his cape just didn't feel right.

"I haven't worn it in years. None of me boys wants it, and Crivy will sock me in the Great Beyond if the moths get to it."

I accepted it graciously and paired it with a woollen vest. Two of its wooden buttons were missing off the bottom but still better than the rest. It wasn't too snug and would keep me warm. All I needed now was a scarf and life would be good.

"Thank you, Gram."

"Yer welcome. Now get the feck off my property."

Klinkle gave me the stink eye on my way out. I didn't wait around in case she decided to berate me. Now, I needed to make some money before securing a way out.

Chapter 9
A Troll on a Mission

Passing cappers now smiled at me; no more glares or stares. I guessed the ugly cape went well with whatever made jovians likeable. Walking through the streets, I noticed a split in capper society. They either dressed in flowing robes decorated with stone and pebble jewellery or stuck to shirts, trousers and overalls. The latter often carried unrecognisable equipment that looked like junk welded together.

Walking through the streets, I realised I wasn't cold, at all. Sure, I was wearing a cloak and a vest, but my face was still exposed. In fact, I felt a comfortable warmth pulsing through my body. When I stood still and focused, it wasn't difficult to figure out where the familiar heat was coming from: the guitar. I recalled its description.

Made from a piece of the Tree of Life, Diya wasn't a piece of inert wood. I got the sense that the guitar was alive. The sensation left my toes and fingertips tingling. It all accumulated in my solar plexus where it was the warmest before circulating around my body. Was this the Mana mentioned in the user interface?

⌈

Congratulations!

You've recognised the existence of Mana. Good job! You're not a closed-minded dolt after all!

Mana Mastery, unlocked!

Mana Mastery:
> The understanding, sensing and manipulation of Mana. Understanding magic is the first step to using

it. You're putting that starting Perception to good use, eh? By following the flow of Mana in your body, you have started your journey towards sensing Mana.

Mana Sense:
You're no longer limited to the natural world, but can now study the Arcane realms as well.

I didn't like the UI's tone. Was the system sentient or had the Cosmics programmed it to annoy people with its snarky tone? Here I was trying to figure out how to survive, and something or someone was taking shots at me.

I checked the Masteries screen. It wasn't blank anymore but now housed a tab labelled 'Active' and another labelled 'Inactive'.

Cooking: Apprentice Rank 5
Mana Wielding: Novice: Rank 0
  -Mana Sense: Novice Rank 1

I wished the system was closer to the RPGs I'd grown up with. Without a help menu or a guide, this would take some time to get used to.

I made a note of my observations. Despite what the system said, it wasn't me detecting Mana that prompted the notifications. Instead, it was me acknowledging it as so. Things were intent-based. Noted. Now that I thought about it, Cooking Mastery didn't unlock until Cook tasted my potato and appreciated it. So others acknowledging my ability would trigger Mastery unlocks too?

Following the same logic, playing the guitar should unlock the respective mastery. I was considering giving busking a shot when the ugly man with the cart caught my attention again.

"Plague cart!" he yelled. "Plague cart heeaaarr! Safe body disposal. No mess, no fuss."

His cart was empty and spotless, but the troll-man seemed determined to fill it. He continued shouting his spiel, slowly walking through the market street ahead. The road displayed the densest concentration of wooden and stone buildings. Crooked and unstable, it looked more like a shantytown than a centre of commerce. Maybe it was a bit of both. As the cart progressed down the street, all capper shoppers filled into nearby shops or disappeared into the alleys while hawkers and stall owners sat back with defeated looks on their face.

"Plaaague cart! A plagued corpse is a bad corpse!" the troll-man continued, looking more and more dejected when no one approached him. "No hassle disposal. You don't ask; I don't tell. Bring your corpses in before they swell!"

He wasn't wearing any personal protective equipment besides an apron over his shorts and shirt. I guessed whatever race he belonged to enjoyed high resistance to cold and disease. Or he was desperate enough to risk the elements and the fear-inducing plague he was shouting about.

Our eyes met again, and he seemed on the verge of breaking into tears. If he didn't look so terrifying, and the cart wasn't a vehicle for plague corpse disposal, I would offer him my sympathy, but maintaining a wide berth was probably for the best.

Then, a trio of capper guards in rough leather and metal armour appeared from out of the alleys. Their spears had strange, bulky contraptions below the spearheads, and similar but mismatched attachments stuck out of their shields as well. Was this the extent of capper tinkering? Considering the shaman's influence, maybe this was more of a magic driven settlement. Though very much like a game, **Game World** wasn't one. So, I reasoned that talking to anyone willing to speak to me was vital to learning more about the world.

"There ain't no plague in Blacknail's Table, boyo," the shortest and stockiest of the guards said. "Yer scaring our citizens. If ye don't stop, I'll put ye in lockup." One of the other guards whispered a few words into their leader's giant, pointed ear. "I mean, the lads will have to kick ye out of town."

"I'm sorry, boys." The troll-man looked embarrassed. "I've been following the Champions of Pestilence around the country. I was sure the plateau was their next destination. I guess I'm early." His shoulders slumped as he looked at the rocky ground disheartened. His feet were bigger than mine; Instead of the tufts of hair, tiny scales covered his. "Not to worry, lads. I'll get out of your hair, maybe return in a few weeks after they've passed through. It's not an easy trade ye know, can't always predict where them lords are heading."

The guards paled, listening to the troll-man speak. Eavesdropping hawkers and stall owners started closing shop, even though most of them hadn't finished setting up. I'd been hoping to spend some more time in this city's safety, not keen to face any rival Champions. But hearing the troll's words, I changed my mind. Getting out as soon as possible took priority. I now had warm clothing. All I needed now was to make a friend who'd help me escape and maybe to travel to a neighbouring settlement with.

"You wouldn't happen to know a good apothecary, would you?" he asked. "There's a parasite going around in Bracken Swamp. I might as well provide them with some aid in the meantime."

"Why don't ye stick around a while?" one of the other guards spoke up. "We could use yer help safeguarding against the coming plague."

"And risk bumping into the Champions of Pestilence?"—he shuddered at the idea—"I clean up after them, not get in the way of them doing their job. Besides, what good is a cemetery troll against a champion? No thank you." The corpse collector clapped the guard's shoulder. He winced at the force and then quickly scurried out of the bigger creature's reach. "Don't worry. I'll be here for the aftermath. You're alright for a capper, mate. If you're not dead by the time I get back, how about we get a drink?"

I watched the guards back away from him, before breaking into a run towards the cliff face where the jail was. I guessed they were off to report to their seniors. For a moment, I felt sympathy for the poor troll. He looked back and forth as everyone stared daggers at him. Most looked at him in fear, others hatred and a handful had pity in their eyes.

Was it his race? Why was he stuck in such a thankless and hated profession? I imagined the world lacked modern medicine and sanitation. The service he was offering was an essential one. Probably due to misinformation, he had arrived at Blacknail's Table ahead of whatever disaster was about to befall the city. Historically, heralds of misfortune and omens were never welcome appearances.

I stayed out of the troll's way as he pushed his cart away from the market street. He looked like the sort that might strike out in anger or grief. Then again, making such an assumption, was I any better than the aelf woman? Better safe than sorry. I waited until he was gone before looking for some way to make money.

Chapter 10
Hide and Seek

With zero coins or whatever backward currency **Game World** used, in my pocket, I probably wouldn't get far. First, I considered busking in the street.

Space turned out to be a commodity nobody wanted to share. Whenever I got close to a workable spot, a nearby capper shooed me away from their ongoing hustle. Not like I had anything to collect coins with anyway. The idea of walking around with cupped hands felt entirely degrading.

Then, I saw a group of face-painted cappers and decided: trying to make money on the streets was a bad idea. Their bone jewellery and ugly staves looked like the classical religious figures of goblin society and set them apart from the other robed citizens. Their blue-orange or white face paints were applied in a variety of shapes, and none of it made them any more attractive. I guessed one of them was the shaman, or they were his followers. Either way, I needed to stay clear of them.

The last thing I wanted was for the insulted father or daughter to strike out at me. I imagined they wouldn't be pleased with my sentence. Antagonising them further, probably wouldn't serve me well either.

I watched them from behind a pile of crates. The mushroom seller that owned it tried to shoo me away, but sticky-fingered capper children kept him too busy. Whenever one of the acolytes got close to a stall, the capper shopkeepers would fawn over them, bowing and showering them with praise. In return for service and goods, the acolytes gave them coins alongside small charms of bone and wood. Some of them vaguely resembled Gor's charm. The acolytes gave merchants selling alcohol a wide berth, focusing their patronage on food and tobacco vendors instead.

Crap. One of them was coming my way. My jovian skin had a healthy tan, and unlike the capper males, the hair on my head wasn't patchy, so, I stood out like a sore thumb. Squatting behind piled boxes of oyster mushrooms, I hoped they wouldn't notice me.

〖 Who knew? Sneaking would come naturally to a little person.〗

Wow. The social justice warriors on Earth would have a field day with the system notifications.

〖
Sneaking Mastery, unlocked!
No, the shadows aren't ready to embrace you quite yet, but improved instincts when trying to remain hidden is always a bonus.
Sneaking Novice: Rank 4
〗

Huh. Unlike Mana Sense, the Mastery didn't start at rank zero. The system did say it would take my natural skills into account. Maybe a childhood filled with hide-and-seek wasn't a waste of time after all. Curious whether it would unlock another Mastery, I stuffed my pockets with what was either cave or chestnut mushrooms. Nope. No such luck.

Maintaining a low crouch, I worked on putting as much distance between the acolytes and me as possible. Much to my disappointment, they were everywhere. Maybe they just finished their post-waking prayers. It didn't matter; I needed someplace to hide.

Sneaking Mastery gained two ranks when I had a near-miss with the one white-faced acolyte. Was he the shaman? Not keen to find out, I turned into a side alley and entered the first tavern I came across. Seeing it was empty, I sighed in relief.

"What are you doing here?" My heart dropped. It was Klinkle. She stood behind the only decent-looking furniture in the room—the bar. "Get out. No more charity for you."

"Just give me a second. Please." I wasn't too big a fan of begging, but the situation was dire.

She glared at me, brows furrowed. Marching past me, she opened the door. "Out. Now!"

"Please," I pleaded. "I'll be out of your hair in no time at all."

"Who're you hiding from?" She peeked out the door. "Is it the rambans?" I was sure she was going to call one of them over. Instead, she slammed her door shut. "You're the foreigner that called Glinga ugly?"

"I know, it's not a nice thing to call—"

"Alright, you can stay," Klinkle said, grinning ear to ear. "About time someone dragged her off her high warg. Just because she's the shaman's daughter, that bitch thinks she can walk around behaving like she's royalty. That girl forgets, the Chief and tinkers still outrank her father."

"Thank you. There's no chance of any of them coming in here, is there?"

"Not at all. The shaman and his rambans only indulge in their powders and pipeweed. They claim alcohol cuts off their link to the spirits." Klinkle shook her head, returning to cleaning mugs. I took a seat on a stool opposite her and carefully leaned my guitar against the bar. "Then they have the gall to tell citizens to avoid the taverns. Not everyone believes them, but the shaman is scary enough for people to stay away until later in the day."

"I don't remember the evening particularly well, but I'm pretty sure I met his daughter in the pub."

"That's the kicker. The shaman and his kin don't follow their own rules." Klinkle slammed one of her mugs down on the bar as she continued, "Every season a merchant from the Bergen Mountains brings over crates of Twergish Firewater. They know very well alcohol doesn't cut off their links. It's a means to control the people. They make a big deal of their spirit singing, but it's just ritualistic Covenant magic, nothing more."

Though angry, Klinkle was giving me a clear picture of capper society. As she carried on with her rant, I learned that there was a clear divide.

There were the shaman and his followers looking to control the masses with their ancient tribal religion, while the tinkers were determined to lead the race into a future with a better understanding of science and the Arcane.

More importantly, I learnt there were seven schools of magic: three of which were Covenant, Creation and Shaping. I wanted to ask her more questions, but she only paused every now and again to catch her breath, and I struggled to get a word in. On the bright side, I got a good idea of the local geography.

Blacknail's Table was set on a plateau. The Bracken Swamps was to the west. It housed several small settlements housing a variety of kobolds, swamp trolls and a handful of wood aelphs scattered around the wilderness. Eldar's Port, a secular commercial hub, was a week by carriage to the south, with several leagues of farmland and villages in between.

Not knowing my status, I needed to give all champions a wide berth. I wasn't aware of whether they had any identifiers or not. There was also the chance of me having a pseudo champion status, despite my lack of a patron. So, there was the likelihood of me being a target in their eyes. Though Eldar's Port was a likely destination or even home for them, I chose it as my destination. A commercial hub felt perfect for my Charisma dumping plans.

"Do you have any work for me?" I asked. During her rant, Klinkle's distaste for me had lessened. So, I took my chance as soon as she stopped for a drink of water. "I don't need much, just room and board until I can afford passage to Eldar's Port."

"Look around," she said, waving at her empty dining room. "Does it look like I can afford a pair of extra hands, let alone give away free food? With the shaman out for your blood, I can understand your desperation to get out of town, but I can't help you. Unless… Do you have any useful Masteries?"

"Mana Sense, Cooking, Sneaking, and Guitar." It wasn't a complete lie. I'd unlock something musical sooner or later. "It's not a lot, I know."

"What have you been doing with your life? I'd expect a jovian to have something related to farming, brewing or even merchant craft. Maybe something magical? What you did with the guitar made no sense. "

Did I just give myself away? I needed to think of an answer, quick!

"I was training in the Bardic Arts." I hoped that it was a real thing. "My master had me focus on the key skills."

"Then why don't you have any speech or lore relevant masteries? I'd expect a Bard to have something akin to Beast Taming at least." She was onto me. Maybe sticking around was a bad idea. I prepared to turn tail and run. "You're a thief, aren't you?" she asked, leaning over the bar at me. "It's fine. I know how you 'cultured' races feel about discussing your status and masteries."

"It's not that," I replied, relieved with her assumptions. "After some trouble with a Champion, I've been trying to lie low. Keeping my cards close to my chest is for the best."

Klinkle sighed. Placing her hands on her hips, she stared at me for a moment. "They didn't release you from prison, did they? Glinga and her da don't forgive or forget."

"You got me." I sighed. "They sentenced me a year of servitude, and this is my day off. I thought I'd try earning some coin for when I get out.

I could tell the 'no' was coming, but then her face softened. She looked between me and the door. Maybe expecting help from her was too much. I had duped her grandfather not too long ago.

"I can't afford to pay you," she said, with a smile which was probably beautiful by capper standards; I couldn't tell. "But, tell you what, if you can play that guitar of yours and get some people in here, I'll share my tips with you. If you're any good, you might make a little for yourself."

It was better than nothing. "You've got a deal."

Klinkle raised an eyebrow when I offered her my hand as if she had never been offered one before. Oh no. Was this not the friendly gesture on **Game World** like it was on Earth? I was starting to hope it wasn't an insult like thumbs-ups were in Greece—or so I'd heard, but then she firmly grasped my hand firmly and shook it.

I couldn't tell whether she'd genuinely warmed up to me, or if **Fact Begins With Fiction** had come into play during our conversation. It didn't matter. I counted this as a minor victory.

"Just remember, thief, if a single coin goes missing from my money box, I'm handing you over to the shaman. They'll ensure you lose your lenient sentence."

Chapter 11
Bar Room Maestro

After three hours of performing, I got the impression that I wasn't the talented, semi-well-known musician I thought I was. I'd been playing songs written by me, and only a handful of cappers had wandered in. When they turned out to be regulars, my confidence found a new low. With a decade of guitar under my belt, I used to think I was pretty damned good. My new harsh reality and Musician Mastery refusing to budge past the ninth Novice rank shattered the illusion.

Klinkle had an apologetic look on her face. I understood it was out of her hands. It was likely that the business wasn't hers. Not willing to sacrifice my pride, I didn't plan on begging her either. Maybe, I'd have put Sneaking Mastery to good use and risk the elements.

As I continued to strum Diya's strings, I detected two distinct energies. The first, we shared. Trying to read it with my Mana Sense, I got nothing. It was colourless, textureless, and neutral. There was nothing extraordinary or exciting about it. I couldn't figure out whether it had any purpose besides existing. The other energy was the one that helped me keep warm. It reminded me of the lush green woodlands outside my parents' house near London and the green fields where I'd walk the family dog, Maya.

Then it occurred to me. I'd never see Maya again. Mum would never push me to focus on my degree. Dad wouldn't ever tell me to put my hobbies on hold until after graduation. Was I a mysterious disappearance that would someday feature on a Twilight Zone reboot? I suppose I'd never know. The thoughts weighed heavily on my chest.

To distract myself, I needed to lose myself to the music. And, it wasn't going to happen while I played the songs I'd written. They always made me conscious of what the audience thought of my melodies and the lyrics. Maybe that was a part of why I never got the reaction I wanted.

"Screw it," I grumbled to myself, abruptly ending the song I'd started only a minute prior. No one so much as looked at me. The only solution was playing a song I'd played a hundred times before. Though I hated myself for it, the first that came to mind was Wonderwall.

Sure, there were dozens of other songs I knew by heart, but I was running out of time. For Klinkle to hold up her end of the bargain, I would need to bring in enough footfall for her to make a profit; which meant, I needed people coming as soon as possible. It left me to wonder whether there was indeed something about the song that I was missing, or it was just the overhyped piece of shit I considered it to be.

So, I started with the riff first. It wasn't a particularly long song, and I needed the room's attention. Repeating the opening melody a few times did the job. Klinkle and more than half her patrons were now looking at me. Satisfied, I looped back to the beginning and started singing.

"Today is gonna be the day when you'll throw your coins to me." They didn't know the real song. Maybe if I added suggestive lyrics, my trait would encourage them to tip more.

It was like letting go. I didn't care whether my audience liked the song or not. It wasn't mine. As a result, all self-consciousness went out of the window. There was only the music and me. I sensed a screen appear in front of my eyes, but I wasn't interested in what it had to say. I felt it minimise itself, waiting for my command.

The circulation of Mana between the guitar and me picked up. It wasn't just the colourless energy but the warm green one as well. As I moved on to the next song, the flow of the latter became overwhelming, and before long, it lulled me into a strange sense of calm.

When I opened my eyes, I wasn't in the tavern anymore. I found myself standing in a thriving woodland and a tree bigger than London's tallest skyscrapers towered over me. Context told me what it was: the

World Tree. It didn't take long for me to guess what the Green Mana was either. The energy belonged to whatever school of Mana governed over life. However, I got the sense that it wasn't just a construct of **Game World**. Did magic exist on Earth as well?

I felt the Mana struggling to break free of the guitar. However, the wood had it trapped inside. Curious, I encouraged it to flow but couldn't figure out how to aid its quest to freedom.

I was playing the final chords of 'Hey Jude' when I noticed the pin-drop silence in the tavern. Opening my eyes, I found the room at maximum capacity. Playing a dozen songs had done the job. Cappers, in all manners of clothing, filled the room. The majority wore clothes similar to Klinkle's trousers, shirt, and coat; but I saw a fair few in overalls carrying ugly, scrappy gadgets. Among them, there were a few robed cappers too. Much to my relief, I didn't see any rambans in the crowd.

"Why'd you stop, jovian?" one of the robed cappers called. "Another one! Play another."

More of the crowd added to his encouragement. Scanning the many smiling faces, I felt happier than I had in a long time. For a moment, I was sure I saw a cat among the many faces, but when I did a double-take, it was gone.

"I need a drink first," I said. "A water maybe?"

"To the Aelph Lord's taint with water!" Klinkle yelled, grinning ear to ear. "For that, ye deserve a real drink, lad."

Then, the room broke into scores of conversations at the same time, and the bar was swarmed with cappers trying to get their orders in. I hoped I'd done enough to earn my room and board.

Though they looked like goblins, capper society didn't share many resemblances to the wild, violent creatures in Earth's fantasy novels. I guessed their budding technology was pulling them out of the tribal dark ages the aelf woman thought they were still stuck in. If anything, they reminded me of Peter Jackson's portrayal of dwarves. Come to think of it.

Their Scottish accents did make sense. The brownies in Celtic legends did include goblins.

Did **Game World** include dwarves? Probably not a pressing concern, but what would they sound like? Vikings?

A slew of notifications popped up, obscuring my vision.

🎵 Better late than never.
Sometimes the best way to grow is to swallow your pride.
Musician Mastery (Guitar and Vocals) has progressed to the Apprentice: Rank 7!
    Control + 1
    Charisma + 1
    Perception + 1
Musician Mastery (Guitar and Vocals) has progressed to Journeyman: Rank 3!
    Control + 1
    Charisma + 1
    Perception + 1
Congratulations!
By advancing two tiers in a Musician Mastery with a single act, you have attracted divine attention.
Achievement unlocked!
Prodigy of the Strings
    Charisma + 2

You have one unassigned stat point. 🎵

They should have made me happy, but the notifications stung. My songs weren't good enough. I only progressed after playing music that wasn't mine. There were more notifications, but I didn't get the chance to study them. There were too many cappers trying to talk to me. I quickly added the extra point to Charisma before turning my attention to them.

It wasn't just cappers in the tavern. There were humans and a few reptilian people as well. They barely stood taller than me, displayed brightly coloured scales, and had horns jutting out from the top of their head. I guessed they were the swamp-dwelling kobolds Klinkle mentioned. They toed the line between pretty and terrifying.

When thinking about kobolds, I imagined humanoid creatures with heads like dragons from Earth's legends and pop culture. Instead, they had disproportionately large skulls in comparison to their body, and their snouts didn't end at a point, but were more rounded. I guessed they needed their massive skulls to support their dense-looking horns.

"That was a marvellous show you put on," said the least goblin-like capper in the room. She had two pint-sized mugs in her hands and offered me one. I accepted it graciously and helped myself to a big gulp. It reminded me of the fermented honey drink Elise's father brewed in his shed. That's right, mead. "That first ballad of yours, what was it called?"

"Wonderwall?" I answered.

If not for her greyish skin and long pointed ears which grew outwards from the sides of her head, I wouldn't have known she was a capper at all. Her skin was smooth and didn't feature warts or scaly textures like the others, and her features were more human than goblinoid. The long braid of red hair hung draped over her shoulder reminded me of the aelphs from race selection.

"Yes, that's the one." Taking my hand, she pulled me away from the hearth to the only empty table in a far corner. "Wonderwall. That's a beautiful name. What's its story?"

I drew a blank. The only bit of trivia I recalled regarding Wonderwall was that the band disliked the song as much as I did.

"I'm Lefa," she said, running a hand up my arm. So, she wasn't particularly interested in an answer. "I'm buying your drinks tonight."

"That's awfully generous of you," I told her, assuring myself I'd stop at two drinks. Though Lefa didn't look horrendous like the rest of the cappers, she was still one of them. My dry spell may have been in its third month, but I wasn't going to end it by sleeping with a goblinoid. "You're in luck then, I'm trying to cut back. Your local brews and I don't mix well."

"Oh, I heard what happened. As stupid as that was, we're glad you did it. Glinga hasn't left her tent since, and we've had some peace and quiet."

I didn't have to order food. The cook brought me a plate of hot stew and crusty bread with the first wave of orders. Afraid it might put me off the meal, I let the meat remain unidentified. Underseasoned and gristly, it wasn't as good as my first meal in **Game World**, but I appreciated the warmth.

"It's Perry by the way." I introduced myself after the first mouthful. Lefa wasn't as surprised as Klinkle had been when I shook her hand. Was it a matter of social status, or was she more used to the gesture due to her non goblin-like appearance? "Travelling bard and maker of bad decisions."

"We don't get a lot of bards on the Table, Perry," she said. "It's refreshing to have one of your kind here. I've been getting sick of the shaman's hymns."

"You don't have a lot of capper bards?"

"Not quite. The shaman doesn't allow outside music, afraid it might interfere with his spirit singing."

Is this what Tolkien's version of Footloose would have been like?

"We do get the occasional musician coming through," Lefa continued. "But, I've never heard anything like Wonderwall before. The words and the melody touched me deep inside."

"It has that effect on people," I said, forcing my eyes not to wander lower. Lefa's breasts were unusually large but still in proportion to her hour-glass frame. No. I could see in her eyes what she wanted, and I wasn't going to give in to my sex-starved urges, especially when it was Wonderwall facilitating my carnal desires.

"So, is this what you do? Travel from city to city playing Wonderwall hoping to enchant the most beautiful girl in town?"

Okay. Lefa wasn't beating around the bush. Was this Charisma at play or was Wonderwall a more powerful song than I gave it credit for. Bloody hell. We weren't even the same species. I needed to diffuse the situation before it got out of hand.

"Not at all. So tell me about Glinga." We needed to change the subject. I pushed my mug away. Temptation reared its ugly head when Lefa traced her fingers up my arm. I hoped squeezing my soft, flabby bicep would put her off me. It didn't. "Why do you and Klinkle hate her so much?"

"She thinks her father's power is hers," Lefa replied, rolling her eyes. "The sad thing is, the shaman doesn't hold as much power as she thinks she does. Not anymore, anyway." Good. She wasn't touching me anymore. So, I egged her on. "Well, since the hobgrems started sharing their knowledge with us and we got our own branch of the Tinker's guild, there is no need for their outdated Covenant magic. We've been lobbying for a link to the Artificers and Mages associations for a while now. Once that's approved, we as a people won't have any need for shamans."

"I imagine his faction are desperately trying to keep that from happening?"

She nodded in response to my question.

I had expected **Game World** to be a wild landscape of monsters and warring champions. Obviously, there was a lot more going on under the surface. If not for the forecasted visit by the Champions of Pestilence, I would have considered sticking around to see where my Charisma would get me.

"Another drink?" Lefa asked when I drained my mug. Given how delicious the beverage was, I couldn't get myself to say no.

Chapter 12
You've Got a Friend in Me

In my dreams, I saw the Tree of Life again. Except, this time I wasn't alone. At first, I could only sense the other two presences. I knew they were there, but my eyes couldn't comprehend whatever form they had assumed.

Approaching its towering height, I pressed my palm against the mossy trunk. It didn't feel like bark or moss should. Instead, it had the same feel as warm, soft skin. I touched my forehead to the bark, and the tree's warm Mana washed over me. Then, the tree started pulling on the energy deep inside me. The pull was strong and threatening. I tried to get away, but the trunk's drag wouldn't let me go. I tried inhaling and exhaling deeply, but I failed to get my racing heart under control. Sure, I was in a dream so I tried waking myself up, but that didn't work either.

When the Tree of Life released me, I staggered backwards and fell on my bottom.

"She's sending you a message," a husky male voice said, making me jump. When I turned around, a short, muscular aelf in baggy brown white trousers and a red vest was standing behind me. "The Tree of Life can take just as easily it gives. She may have granted you a fragment of her power, but it's not something to be taken lightly."

I didn't need to scan him with my Mana Sense to know. He was divinity. The air around him rippled with every syllable that left his lips, and my eyes struggled to hold his gaze.

"What makes you think I'm taking it lightly?" I asked.

"Just conveying the message." He stared at me for a moment. "I know you have questions on your mind. Why don't you ask them?"

Maybe he was a Cosmic or something similar, and he was using this as an opportunity to flex his power. Unwilling to give him the satisfaction, I held my tongue. When the man walked towards me, the ground under my feet vibrated, and the wind whistled. He placed a hand on my shoulder, making every bone in my body hum. Though his attempt at intimidation was successful, I didn't flinch. Instead, I looked him in the eye and smiled.

"I told you, he's an interesting one," a second voice said. It was female and husky. It would have been enticing in a mellow way, like the scent of a freshly opened bottle of Belgian wheat beer, if I hadn't recognized the speech pattern.

"Well, I had to see for myself. You don't have the best reputation when it comes to telling the truth, do you, Maka Dee?"

A spider as big as me rappelled down from the enormous tree's branches. I don't know why, but it didn't frighten me as much as the man.

"That hurts, love. It really does." Maka's presence helped sharpen the blurry environment that was my dreamscape. "Here I am, trying to help you out of the goodness of my spider heart, and you're still dwelling on the past."

"We can never be sure about you, Maka Dee," the man said, and my bones hummed again. Why was the sensation so familiar? "You have a history of taking more than you give."

"That stings, Sang. It really does. I thought we were all friends."

"If you're done being mysterious, I'd like to know what's going on," I said, my eyes focused on Maka's giant spider form. "Where did you go? I didn't expect your assistance to end so soon."

"You too?" A momentary chill filled the air as Maka voiced her displeasure, but the Tree of Life's warmth overwhelmed it almost straight away. "What have I ever done to deserve this?"

"You're a trickster," Sang said.

"Lies!" Maka exclaimed, humour returning to her tone. "You know I'm all about knowledge and stories. Sure, I might use what I know to get what I want. Perhaps I like to have some fun at everyone's expense while at it. By my children's webs, I might fool you from time to time, but that doesn't make me a trickster."

"Tall tales and part truths would be more accurate. You just described a trickster, Maka Dee. Don't deny it."—Sang turned to me—"Wouldn't you agree?"

"I don't particularly want to get involved in… whatever this is," I said. "Could either of you please tell me why I'm here?"

Sang looked at Maka expectantly, but the giant spider only waved her pedipalps and fangs. Perhaps she intended the action to appear endearing, but it appeared more terrifying than nice.

"Do you want a champion or not, Sang?" She finally asked, shedding light on the purpose of our meeting. "He's not been in the Verse three days, and he's a Journeyman Musician. Not to forget all the hearts he has won with his melodies. Don't you want to try to ascend the ladder once again?"

"You know I do, Maka Dee." Sang sighed, and the vibrations stopped. "Unfortunately, this jovian and I aren't a good match. I need someone whose sole focus is the music. His isn't. I gave him a boon for his achievement, and he hasn't yet looked at my gift." Sang looked between us. "He lacks direction and purpose. If you ask me, he's much better suited to—"

"Well, no point in us continuing this meeting then," Maka said, cutting Sang off. "I was hoping you'd be more grateful, Sang. You could've been great together."

Consciousness came with a splitting headache. The comfort of the World Tree and the two oppressing presences were gone. Instead, I felt a rough but soft mattress under me, and a smooth warmth pressed into my side. It was Lefa.

Memories of the night came flooding back. Loud images punctuated a whole lot of blurriness. Two drinks turned into four, and after a slurred round of singing, we had been all over each other. I recalled Lefa's deep sigh when I entered her, and the taste of her breasts. Despite her discomfort, she had welcomed me hungrily.

Maybe Samantha was right. I did have a drinking problem. At least, I hadn't slept with a full-blooded capper. I recalled Lefa telling me about her mother's human and wood aelph heritage. It explained why she didn't look like the rest of her people. At the same time, I was curious why Lefa's mother would ever pair up with a capper. Did she take advantage of me? Considering my history, probably not.

Carefully lifting her arm off me, I rolled out of bed. I almost hurled as soon as I was upright. The change in orientation was much too jarring. Now that I was in a world filled with magic, there had to be a spell or some alchemical brew to help with hangovers.

"You're not planning on sneaking out, are you?" Lefa asked, bleary-eyed.

Okay. Lefa wasn't hideous by the light of day. Her skin's green was more luscious than sickly, and her teeth were almost all perfectly straight. The wood aelph blood showed but her jutting ears and hooked nose gave away her goblinoid heritage.

"Not at all," I lied, pulling my clothes on. "Just going to go get some tea..."

"Good. That was my first. I won't be happy if you run away."

Oof. I deserved a punch in the gut. Given her clothing, I was sure Lefa had no connection to the shaman or the tinkers. So, I didn't have to worry about getting thrown in prison again. Despite her loveliness, I wasn't in the emotional space for a relationship. Not only did I still need to get used to this new world, but the wounds left in me by Samantha needed more time to heal.

"I'd never do that." Despite the hangover, I flashed her my best smile. "See, I'm leaving my guitar here. A bard goes nowhere without his instrument."

I'd let her down easy when she joined me downstairs. Hopefully she would understand. I sure hoped no capper father would force me into a crossbow wedding. I wouldn't have a choice if they did. Until my sentence ended or I found a way out of town, I'd have to do whatever the cappers wanted of me.

There were still cheerful voices in the common room downstairs. They were much too loud, and it hurt my head, but I really did need to quench my thirst. Even though my instincts told me to run, I intended to do the right thing. I'd stick around and pay the price of my actions. My mum raised me better than that.

"Maka, I could use your help right now," I mumbled. Some advice or guidance.

Recalling Sang's words, I pulled up my notifications.

⌈ You may choose a Mastery specific perk for achieving the Journeyman rank.

A divine entity has upgraded your choice of perks.

Earworm:
> Your music refuses to fade from memory. The effects of your songs last much longer; duration increases with Charisma.

Arcane Chords:
> Weaving magic into your music not only comes naturally to you, but is now more Mana efficient.

Play by Ear:
> You have a knack for mimicking all manner of sound and are now pitch-perfect.

⌋

The decision wasn't an easy one. At some point or another, every musician wishes he were pitch-perfect. Some of the greatest composers and musicians were blessed with the gift. Mozart, Handell, Michael Jackson. I would love to be one of them. However, I needed to be practical. I needed tools for survival and power.

Earworm needed **Facts Begin With Fiction**. Arcane Chords required I learn magic to be of any use. Both were tempting. Given my Pacifist trait and my race limiting my magical potential, Earworm should have been the obvious pick, but I was still hopeful. There had to be some sort of magic I could learn and excel at.

After some thought, I chose Arcane Chords. None of the options would help me anytime soon, so I went with the one that had the most potential. My Mana Sense confirmed, both Diya and I had wells of magic inside of us. Sooner or later, I would find uses for them. Besides, I recalled the green Mana's desperation to break free. Maybe now I'd be able to see what it wanted to do.

𝄆 **Identification:**
    First Name: Peregrin   **Last Name:** Kanooks
    Race: Jovian   **Patron:**—
    Condition: Dehydrated   **Mana Core:** Full
Stats:
    Brawn: 1   **Control:** 8
    Mind: 3   **Arcana:** 1
    Charisma: 15   **Perception:** 8
Traits:
    Pacifist
    Fact Begins With Fiction
    Arcane Chords
𝄇

Pleased with my new Charisma and Control scores, I headed down the stairs. My parched throat drove me towards the bar. On making eye contact, Klinkle shot me a big grin. As soon as I got to the bar, she placed six silver coins on the counter.

"Excellent take, if you ask me," she said. "People mostly left you coppers, but I used them up making change. So, I rounded up. Most families would consider themselves lucky to make that in a week."

"Thank you." I slipped them into my cape's inner sleeves. "How much did I drink?" I asked as she poured me a mug of water. I grabbed it without hesitation and downed the liquid. The ice-cold temperature stung my belly but at the same time felt wonderful.

"You have a problem," Klinkle told me. "You suck at saying no, don't you?"

I passed the mug back for her to refill. "I don't know how capper society works. Do I have to marry her now?"

Klinkle looked past me at the few remaining patrons. "Chieftain Grog! Perry here wants to know whether he can marry your daughter?"

I froze in my seat. Why didn't Lefa tell me she had spawned from the massive capper's seed? More importantly, how the hell did I miss him in the bar? I hadn't seen a capper bigger than him yet. He looked at me with his brows furrowed. Standing up from his chair, Grog marched up to me and placed a massive hand on either side of the bar.

"You want to marry my daughter?" He asked, nostrils flared. "You want to know whether you, an incarcerated halfling, can marry my daughter?"

"Da, leave him alone?" Lefa yelled from the top of the stairs. She stomped down the stairs with the sheets wrapped around her like a strapless dress. "I don't want you scaring away another one!"

"Another one? You told me, I was your first!" I grimaced as soon as the words left my mouth. Lefa's current state was a dead giveaway, her hair stuck out like a wild man around her pretty face, and she had nothing on but the sheets wrapped around her torso.

Grog looked between her and I, before bursting into laughter. Klinkle and the cappers followed suit. "Her first? Her first jovian maybe."

"Da!" Lefa laughed. "Why do you have to ruin my fun?"

"Listen here, son," Grog said, placing a heavy hand on my shoulder. "I don't know how they do things where you're from, but we're warriors.

Capper blood runs hot. We fight, we drink, and then we go to bed with whoever is willing. And no, you aren't going to marry my daughter."

Lefa giggled, placing her hands on her hips. "You're handsome and have a good voice, Perry, but we just met," she said. "You didn't really think this meant we're betrothed, did you? You were good, lad, but not that good. Silly jovian."

"It's okay honey. They're village folk. Jovians take joy in growing crops and rearing cattle. Don't scare the boy." Grog returned his attention to me. "Besides, my first daughter won't marry a skinny halfling that's never held a weapon. I want mighty grandchildren that can shoot arrows from a sprinting warg. You're stocked up on Whoopsie Brew, right?"

"Of course, Da! I'm not ready to lose my curves."

I didn't know whether to feel relieved or insulted. With dusk approaching, Cook would need me in the kitchens. The breakfast porridge wouldn't stir itself. I left the pub not long after, with the pair still laughing their heads off. Maybe it wasn't the worst of outings. I got a day away from the prison, won a cloak in a bet and got laid for the first time in over three months. To top it all off, I had three new Masteries, several new stat points and a new perk. Not a bad outing at all.

Chapter 13

Halfling Cook

My night with Lefa added to my infamy.

Now, I was more than the gutsy jovian that had sung about Glinga's ugly mug. I had bedded the prettiest capper in town, Grog's daughter. Gor told me, she never went to bed with cappers. The chieftain kept hoping she'd pick a member of his war band, but she only went for members of other races.

Apparently, the last jovian to visit Blacknail's Table had spurned her advances. Now, he no longer ventured to Blacknail's Table to sell his spiced ale. Lefa had bedded humans, aelves, aelphs, hobgrems, dwez—some sort of dwarven people and even tried it on with kobolds. Unfortunately, she had failed on her last escapade due to their reptilian physiology. Apparently, instead of condemning her carnal appetites, Grog took pride in his daughter's affairs.

The chieftain claimed Lefa had not just inherited his appetite, but her mother's too. Considering how Hruk described it, wood aelphs were **Game World**'s hippies. They hugged trees, danced naked under the moonlight and practised free love. No wonder **Game World**'s citizens took advantage of them.

The experience, on the whole, proved humbling. I'd be lying if I didn't admit it, but when I woke up next to Lefa, my first instinct had been to run. At the tender age of twenty, I still had a lot to figure out. Marriage was the last thing on my mind. After the breakup, Samantha and I met to exchange the belongings we had left at each other's apartments. I remembered what she had told me.

"You're scared of commitment."

"Oh yeah, that's a great excuse," I had replied. "Just because I'm not willing to spend every hour of every day with you, I'm scared of commitment?"

"Well, I needed you, and you weren't there," Samantha had said.

"I'm sorry. Did my me-time drive you into the arms of another man?" I remembered wanting to shout, but I had managed to keep the volume down. Instead, the words had come out cold and venomous. "We studied together, went to the gym together. Hell, I spent most nights a week at your place. Then, when I took a couple of hours to do my own thing, you mounted the guy that's supposedly like a 'little brother' to you?"

I remembered Samantha staring daggers at me, not saying anything. For a moment, I thought I had seen her lip quiver, but then Samantha folded her arms under her breasts.

"Well?" I recalled getting impatient. "Aren't you going to say anything?"

"No," she had answered. "You've already made up your mind about me being a bitch. Nothing I say is going to change that."

Enough of that.

After four more days of me working in the kitchen, Cook had taken the day off. Gor stuck around supervising me to ensure I didn't try anything. Still, I had full control of the kitchen. As a part-time worker, I had never enjoyed the opportunity before.

Cook didn't trust me not to sully his good name. So, he'd made a game and root vegetable stew the night before and left me to make the day's bread and heat the meal for dinner. Easy enough. Unlike Cook's preference, I made the dough before going to bed.

The following morning, when I woke up in the storeroom, it had doubled in size. I divided the dough into six and shaped them into long loaves. After placing them on floured trays to leaven once again, I stoked the woodstove. It took much too long to heat up; a lot went into a day's work. While the prisoners' dinner cooked, I needed to prepare their breakfast.

Once the stove had heated up, I made a big pot of oatmeal with water, dried mushrooms, and wild herbs. A smaller batch, with milk and blackberry jam, was reserved for the staff and us working inmates. The cappers didn't keep cattle: due to the cold climate and rocky soil, very little grew in the region. Feeding livestock beyond the rare goat was a challenge, so the city got most of its meat through hunting and trading with the swamp dwellers to the west. However, dairy imports *did* come through dangerous trade routes from the Eldar Plains, making milk, butter, and cheese luxury imports far too good for the prisoners. I relished my contraband breakfast every morning; privileges of being kitchen staff.

Hruk arrived just as I finished loading a pot of oatmeal onto the meal cart. It surprised me how relaxed the prison staff were around us working prisoners. We had access to knives, meat mallets, fire, and long poles—odd that they didn't seem to worry we'd turn against them.

"Why are they so relaxed around us?" I asked when Gor left with the breakfast cart. "Aren't they worried we might steal some contraband and use it against them?"

"Look at us," he said. "You're a jovian, and I'm probably the weakest capper in town."

"There's got to be more than that, could the system possibly give them any information about us?"

"I've never thought about it. Why? You planning a prison break?"

"Isn't that every prisoner's fantasy?"

"Not mine," Hruk answered. "I have food, a roof over my head, and work to keep me busy. There's no work for a scribe in Blacknail's Table and getting work outside capper settlements is next to impossible."

Come to think of it, none of the prison staff searched me when I came home from my day off. There had to be some sort of security measure ensuring we wouldn't turn against the prison staff.

So, once Hruk left me alone, I explored the facility. I didn't have access to parts of the facility exclusively for cappers, but there was still a lot to explore. With my increased Perception, I spotted several new details but nothing out of the ordinary. The rarity of prison guards had initially perplexed me. Then again, the part of prison dedicated to outsiders didn't need many guards. It only held three prisoners: the aelf woman, the man and me.

There was no secret viewing room or scrappy gadgets attached to the halls. Security couldn't be this relaxed. Then it occurred to me, **Game World** and Earth weren't the same. While stuck looking for something physical, I hadn't considered magical surveillance or safeguards. So, I tapped into my Mana Sense.

The new sense lit up the world around me. Unfortunately, it stopped an arm's length from my body. However, the first second of it being active gave me more information than the half hour I'd spent scouring the corridors. Standing in a doorway, I sensed glowing wisps of energy lining the frame.

A screen popped up, displaying the Mastery ranking up. A lot had changed over the past couple of days, so I checked the menu.

Cooking: Apprentice: Rank 5
Mana Wielding: Novice Rank 1*
    -Mana Sense: Novice Rank 3*
Musician: Journeyman Rank 3
Sneaking: Novice Rank 4

I saw shimmering wisps of purple, pink and ruby. They danced around golden circles lined with runic symbols. None of it made sense. Breaking out of prison wouldn't be easy until I understood what the magic did—I needed someone who could give me more information, and I knew just who to approach.

I needed to wait until Gor's day off before I could proceed. Grog still hadn't delivered on his promise to provide more Mind Magic Resistant totems. So the middle-aged capper left me his locket made of bone and hair. I pricked my finger on the totem's jagged end to activate it, expecting a rush of power or a glow, but I felt and saw nothing. Bloody hell, would I have to wait until someone assaulted me with Mind Magic to know whether the totem was functional or not?

I needed Hruk's help to carry the food cart through the facility. He had me wait outside the capper-only section of the prison while delivering breakfast to the inmates. Then, he did the same while I met with the aelf woman. The prospect of Mind Magic terrified him. I'd be lying if I said it didn't scare me too, but cowering in fear wouldn't get me anywhere.

"Are you reconsidering my offer, jovian?" the aelf woman asked as soon as she saw me. I felt a probing energy assault my psyche but an invisible force flared from the locket, repelling it.

I responded to her question with another, "Do aelves not need to eat? Can you sustain yourself on dungeon air and good looks?" The woman accepted the bowl of stew with a slice of bread and attacked it hungrily. I gave her a moment to eat before continuing, "This life debt. How does it work?"

The aelf didn't answer my question. Instead, her eyes flashed, and a blue screen appeared in front of me.

⌈ Lily Dawnstar has offered you a life debt.
If you help Lily escape her cell, she will be in your service until she saves your life or the debt is repaid.

As long as Lily is indebted to you, she may not betray you or actively put you in harm's way.

However, nothing is stopping her from finding a non-violent escape from the pact. You're really out to make a splash, aren't you? ⌋

"Last time, you got dragged away before the system registered my offer. You planning a prison break, jovian?"

"The name's Perry," I told her, "and of course. Much like you, the less time I spend here the better. The Champions of Pestilence are on their way to Blacknail's Table."

"That is bad news," Lily said. "Dwez scrot! I really would rather not be in a prison when a plague hits. What's the plan?"

"None yet. There's magic lining every major doorway and junction connecting different parts of the facility." She nodded along to my explanation as if it were common knowledge. While I spoke, she sauntered over to the bars. I liked the way her hips moved. "Could you disable them?"

"I'm a Mind Mage, not an Enchanter, unfortunately. That's not my forte." Lily reached through the bars, grabbed the back of my head and pulled me in for a kiss. For a moment, I tried to pull away but didn't resist for long. That was a damned good kiss. Clearly, such intimacy was her forte. Then, I felt a tug around my neck and grabbed her wrist.

"I'm not that easy to manipulate," I said, snatching the locket out of her grip. My right hand curled into a fist, but I stopped myself before throwing the punch. I'd never hit someone of the opposite gender outside of Martial Arts tournaments. Pacifist trait or not, I bloody well wasn't going to start now. "We've just met, and you're already trying to violate the life debt."

Sighing, she returned to her cot. "The life debt doesn't come into play until you directly or indirectly help me escape this cell. Seems like we'll only get out if I enchant one of the prison staff..."

"There has to be another way." I backed away from the bars. "These cappers are good people. I don't like the idea of you using one as a puppet."

"Think about it," she replied. "Take some time. Me taking control of our beloved jailor is the best way out I can think of."

I didn't like her idea. Ever since I found out about the existence of Mind Magic, its morality had me concerned. And like a certain over quoted saying goes, "with great power came with great responsibility." Lily didn't just want to peek into Gor's mind. By taking the bracelet, she wanted to turn him into a puppet and use the jovial capper to facilitate our escape.

I recalled what he and Warden had told me about her. Lily had enough power to mind control an entire squad of cappers. Once she repaid the life debt, she could just as easily do the same to me. Long story short, I couldn't trust her.

The human prisoner accepted the stew and bread without me having to say a word. He shot me a knowing smile, probably having heard my conversation with Lily. Much to my surprise, he didn't ask me to include him in any escape plans.

Chapter 14
Oh! I Want to Be Free

After growing up glued to a screen and controller, **Game World** had everything I could ever want. Stats, Magic, Traits. I could've made it work despite the Pacifist trait, but why did the Devourer of Worlds have to put me in prison? What a bitch move. Sure, Boots had tried to help, but Maka had proven herself to be a flake. I didn't know what she was up to, but nothing she had done so far helped me out of my predicament.

In games, I always picked one of two builds. My first choice would always be the assassin; I sucked at it due to my impulsive tendencies and lack of patience. Still, sniping a target with a bow or getting a satisfying stab from the shadows always got my heart pumping. If not that, I'd go for meaty mage-type characters that abused spell-vamp items or magic.

In **Game World**, I'd probably pick the latter even though it was my second choice. As a stealth reliant individual, I didn't trust myself to not make an impulsive move and get myself killed. Unfortunately, neither dream would come to fruition. I did have Sneaking, but I wouldn't be using it to kill anyone. To be honest, I didn't have the stomach to kill anyone. On Earth, I used to be short and skinny as well. Mum had enrolled me in Shotokan Karate so I could stand up to bullies. Even though I would often get to the semi-finals in competitions, when it came to real-life fighting, I'd always pull my punches. The thought of seriously hurting someone scared me.

None of that mattered now. The crypt troll said he'd return in a few weeks. The Champions of Pestilence would be in Blacknail's Table any day now. I needed to get out as soon as possible.

As I continued working in the kitchens, Cooking Mastery eventually progressed to the Sixth Apprentice rank. All my Masteries, except for Musician, experienced a little growth as I continued to explore the prison looking for some way to escape undetected. If my captors believed I was still in the building, maybe no one would think to look for me in the city until I was far from it. Then again, after my performance at Klinkle's and bedding Lefa, most of the city probably knew a fair bit about me.

"What's with the human prisoner?" I asked Hruk one afternoon. Cook left us alone to take a nap while we did a deep clean of the kitchen. "I've seen him twice now, and he doesn't talk. What's he in for?"

"Angering the shaman," Hruk answered. "He arrived in Blacknail's Table a month ago, claiming to be a scrimshaw and diviner. At first, the rambans went crazy for his bone trinkets and artwork. Then, one morning he started telling people about having a vision of the future. Only the shaman can look into the future. They denounced him as a blasphemer and accused him of seeding chaos before throwing him in here."

"That's pretty stupid, isn't it? What kind of vision did he have?"

"He claimed that a champion would soon arrive in the city and cause great violence and sorrow. True or not, people don't want to hear that. We have scouts out there to warn us if any champions approach our borders."

All of a sudden, the man's knowing smile made a whole lot of sense. Was he talking about the Champions of Pestilence, or me? I had always thought astrology, clairvoyance and diving to be scams. In **Game World** atheism would involve blind ignorance. If spirits, Cosmics and deities existed, people with the ability to peek into the future probably walked among us too.

My following day off came at Grog's request. He'd not long returned from a raid and wanted to spend a lively evening at the tavern. So he wanted the only bard in town attending the gathering to provide music for his war party.

Cook expressed his displeasure regarding the request. He'd planned on taking the day off but didn't have it in him to stand up to the chieftain.

After helping him with breakfast, I headed out into the city. It had gotten colder. Jovian cold resistance seemed limited to the feet and lower leg. Despite Gram's cape and jumper, my entire body trembled as I trudged through the town.

On my way there, I decided to pay the stables a visit. I needed to study the gate and plan an exit strategy. Maybe, if I saw any merchants leaving town, I could bribe them for a lift or stowaway in their cart unnoticed.

Blacknail's Table had not long woken up. Most of the shops were closed, stalls and food carts only beginning to set up. There were barely any cappers around. I spotted the occasional human and kobold milling about, but that was it. A few amongst them waved at me, and I waved back. None of their faces was familiar, but I guessed we had become acquainted during my evening at Klinkle's.

Following the main road towards the city walls, I walked through the Tinkers' district. Much like their contraptions, the buildings they inhabited looked like they were made from scrap hastily bound together. On Earth, a few of them would probably count as modern junkyard art. It was like weaving through a woodland full of nettles where a scratch could result in tetanus.

I spotted a half-capper brushing snow off his cart. Its side had a cartoonish likeness of his face painted onto it with a milk moustache. The sign below it read: Milky Pete's Dairy Farm. Of the vehicles exiting the city, only his cart appeared to have room for me to hide in. Unfortunately, a one-eyed bear of a man stood screaming at him like a petulant child while the farmer faced him bored and expressionless.

"What do you mean you won't give me a ride out of town?" He growled. "You know who I am? You don't say no to the great Cosmic Penguin's Champion."

"No money, no ride," Milky Pete replied. "You want me to go out of my way, which will make me late getting home. I ain't adding a day to my journey, especially with that attitude of yours."

"But I'm a champion! You have to help me. It's the rules! Haven't you heard of my exploits?"

"What rules?" The half-capper laughed, and the one-eyed bear man's face reddened. "Sure, I've heard of you, Thorne. Weak and powerless, relying on divine intervention to solve your problems. You don't scare me."

Thorne squealed like a pig, stamping his feet like a spoilt brat denied his ice cream. "I'm a champion, and you'll do as I say. Take me to Eldar's Port!"

"Go cry to your patron." Milky Pete poked Thorne's chest with a long skinny finger. "You don't scare me."

The second Milky Pete poked him again, a flash of light illuminated the stable's darkness. Holy hell. Was that a chubby little penguin I saw? It honked and squawked, making the poor farmer jump.

"See! I'm a champion!" The bear-shaped man looked mighty proud of himself. "Will you help me now?"

Milky Pete appeared dazed, as if he had no control over his body anymore. Moving like a marionette, he waved Thorne over. With an entitled grin, Thorne climbed into the cart, and it rolled towards the gate. The penguin shifted its attention to me, and for a second there was worry in its eyes. Was I not supposed to see what had just happened? Right. Maybe Cosmics weren't allowed to influence **Game World** directly, and that's precisely what it had done. The creature honked again and disappeared in a puff of smoke, leaving me unsure of what to do next.

During their exchange, Thorne and Milky Pete had drawn a fair bit of attention. Many pairs of eyes had met mine as well. Among them was an armoured capper guard, riding a massive yet simultaneously ugly canine. In proportion to me, the creature was as large as a horse. It had shaggy fur no different from a wolf's but had a hyena-like face and giant fangs no different from a sabre-tooth tiger's. That had to be a warg. As soon as the rider egged his creature onwards in my direction, I turned heel and headed towards Klinkle's pub. No point in looking for an escape vehicle when my captors could run us down in no time.

"Yer the lad with the wall ballad, aren't yee?" An elderly capper stopped me on the road. She carried a bouquet of bright pink tulip-like flowers. I peeked over my shoulder. The warg rider had followed me from the gaze. He appeared relaxed, but his mount maintained a healthy distance. "That was a lovely song, laddie. Reminded me of the day I met me husband."

"I'm glad you enjoyed it, Miss."

She burst into an almost-girlish giggle and smacked my forearm playfully. "You're as charming as they come," she said. "Has anyone ever told you that?"

"Not enough I'm afraid," I answered, putting on my best smile. I could feel the warg and its riders eyes burning a hole through the back of my head. "I'm on my way to Klinkle's now. Why don't you come around and have a listen?"

"Oh no, I still have a lot of flowers to sell." Then, she picked a flower out of her bouquet and tucked it into a frayed stitch near my collar. "Here. If ye have a special lass in your life, give her one of these. Won't just loosen her legs but win her heart too."

The capper's statement jolted concerns of the guard out of my mind. I almost forgot how open their society was on the subject of sex. On Earth, I'd never have expected to hear such a statement from someone old enough to be my grandparent. Then again, my parents were immigrants. Born in the old country, during a different time; their parents had a more orthodox way of thinking. I remember hearing stories of everyone protesting their marriage due to the difference in caste. Long story short, they were old school, and these almost tribal goblinoids came across as very progressive.

"Thank you," I told her before continuing towards my destination.

On arriving, I found half a dozen wargs standing around outside the tavern's entrance. Growing up, we always had dogs in the house. My father taught me how to care for canines; how to groom them and when it was required to force medicine down their throats. So, I was familiar with the odours that followed dogs. However, I wasn't ready for the assault on my senses when I got near them.

While the cappers didn't live up to the goblin stereotype, their mounts definitely did. I almost gagged at the smell of rotting meat when the closest beast's horrid breath hit my face. The warg's big tongue hung out the side of its mouth as it seemingly smiled at me. Chief's mount, I guessed. Not only was it the biggest, but the saddle on its back had polished steel guards on the front and back. As ugly as the beast appeared, looking at its friendly expression, I couldn't help but pet it.

That's right. The sweet point between the ears always worked. The big guy closed his giant yellow eyes, and a pleasure-filled rumble sounded from deep within his throat. I ducked when the warg tried to lick me. He took it as a game and jumped at me. It was then I noticed how my speed and reaction time had changed over the past week.

A few days ago, I would have stumbled and fallen on my bottom, but now I had no trouble adjusting my landing. It was the increase in my Control stat. Waving goodbye to the warg, I entered Klinkle's, and friendly shouts and hooting welcomed me.

Chapter 15

Wish You Were Here

Despite it being early in the evening—morning for cappers, Klinkle's tavern didn't have a single free table. Armed and armoured cappers alongside humans occupied most of the room. They came in all shapes and sizes: short, tall, round, stick-like, and a few combinations that didn't make a whole lot of sense.

Among them, I spotted a handful of kobolds and a couple of me-sized human-like individuals. Unlike jovians, they had rounded ears and pastel-coloured facial hair. I couldn't tell whether their polished, bald heads were a life-style choice or natural. Like capper tinkers, they carried strange metal gadgets. However, instead of scrappy, theirs had a more sleek and well-crafted appearance.

Before I could investigate them further, the room noticed my presence and cheered. "Wonderwall lad is here!" Grog yelled, and a pair of bony cappers wearing hide armour swept me off the floor. Their scaly palms scraped my skin, but I managed to hide my discomfort. Considering their rough appearance, I worried complaining would encourage more manhandling. "What took you so long lad?"

"I'm sorry, Chief," I said, scrambling to think up an excuse. "I didn't think you'd be here this early. Since I'm not going anywhere any time soon, I thought to have a look around my new home."

"Sure." Grog grinned. He probably had an exceptionally high Perception score. I'd need a lot more Charisma to pull off such a lame lie. Maybe **Fact Begins With Fiction** would help me out? "Nice flower you got there. Trying to look good for a lass, are ya?"

"You got me." That would've made a much more convincing story. "I didn't just bathe because Cook made me." I raised my voice so the other patrons could hear. "With so many beautiful women around, I need to look my best, don't I?"

"Someone get a drink for the pretty boy!" a scarred warrior with half a nose yelled. He had his arms draped around two capper women. Right. In a warrior based society, my softer boyish looks probably didn't count for much. "He smells too fresh. A couple of pints should fix that!" He won a fair number of laughs from the crowd.

I could barely see past the patrons standing around the bar, talking or trying to order a drink. Wishing Klinkle a good evening would have to wait. I didn't expect to share her tips a second time, but looking at the crowd, I hoped to walk away with more money than last time.

"Chief, while I have you here, could I maybe have a word?" I asked, just as he was turning away.

"Sure thing, lad. What is it?" The over-sized cappers speech had lost its previously jovial tone. Did he not buy my story?

"On my last day off in the market, I saw a crypt troll with a plague cart—"

"Don't worry your pretty little head about that," Grog told me in a hushed voice. "I have high-Perceptions scouts posted all around the mountains, and the shaman has his spirits patrolling the lands too. If any entity as powerful as the Champions of Pestilence gets close, I'll know about it. There's a reason why I'm chieftain, lad." He clapped me on the back, almost knocking me over. "I respect your intention, but don't mention this again."

Grog walked away without elaborating his order. As the Capper Chieftain, he didn't need to. Of course. I wasn't the only one who had heard the conversation between the guards and the corpse collector. More than one source must have reported the information to Grog. He claimed to have the situation under control, but I saw it as hubris. Sure, Grog and his people had lived in **Game World** much longer than me, but a threat with a name like 'Champions of Pestilence' deserved more attention. Instead, I watched the chieftain walk up to a buxom human and offer to buy her a drink.

After scanning the room properly, I spotted a lot more women in the tavern: not just cappers, but humans as well. Last time, engrossed in music and then Lefa, I hadn't been paying attention. Now, I got the chance to see how progressive Blacknail's Table was. Not only were there men with multiple women, but women making out with more than one man at a time as well. The focus of each group seemed to be capper warriors, regardless of their gender. Despite the occasional one night stand, I liked to think of myself as a one-woman guy. Though I didn't want anything resembling a relationship, I found myself scanning the room for Lefa.

Then a familiar skinny capper thrust a pint of mead into my hands. "Hruk!" I exclaimed. "What are you doing here?" For once the skinny capper wore more than just trousers. His mismatching boots appeared too big for his green feet, and his jumper hung down to his knees.

"Klinkle needed help for the evening and the chief volunteered me for the role," he answered, sounding worse for wear. While lively and sweet in the prison building, Hruk appeared disturbed and uncomfortable in the tavern. "The lasses have got their eye on you."

Hruk nodded at the corner of women from all races. Quite a few of them had their eyes trained on us.

"I think they're looking at you, mate." Smiling, I raised my mug at the little gathering. Most of them returned the gesture.

"You don't have to do that, Perry," Hruk said. "I've long gotten used to the idea, women of my kind don't like me. On the other hand, you bedded Lefa, and she didn't have one negative thing to say about you. That, and the flower you have makes you a very interesting prospect."

I never expected a flower would make me so desirable. Different land, different rules. Unfortunately, none of them piqued my fancy. I had zero sexual interest in full-blooded cappers, and even though I found some of the human women attractive, I didn't want to go to bed with them. I worried the difference in size would make things awkward. Maybe I was overthinking it, but even the shortest of them had more than a foot on me. I'd consider it if my head reached as far as their shoulder.

"You can never tell what someone finds attractive, Hruk," I said.

Over the last few days, I had developed a liking for the little guy. Maybe having someone shorter around helped me feel better about my new stature. Perhaps the close proximity and my homesickness had created a void in my heart, and Hruk's company helped me forget it. We were in the same boat after all. Instead of continually looking for a way out of his incarcerated life, Hruk had embraced it. So, I took it on myself to help him feel better.

"Where I come from, the tall, muscular and handsome get the best women. However, there are large groups of people dedicated to the worship of short, fat, or hairy. We call them kinks or fetishes. No matter what you look like, there will be someone attracted to you—given you have personal hygiene and treat people with respect, of course. Chances are there is someone in this room that likes your look. You just need to get out of your shell and get over your self-pity. Once you stop thinking of yourself as lesser than others, the prospects will show themselves."

Hruk's face brightened. "Do you have a kink too?"

"Not particularly. However, I have a soft spot for pale women with dark hair in high ponytails. If they wear thick-rimmed glasses, that's a nice bonus. My people call it a librarian fetish." I left out the bit about pencil skirts since it wouldn't make sense to him.

"Jovians are weird," he commented before an armoured capper ordered him to fetch more drinks.

I didn't like how the other cappers spoke to him. It was probably the many years of such treatment that turned him into a pushover. I needed to divert their attention. So, I pushed through the crowd to the front of the room. As soon as I strummed the first chord, several pairs of eyes drifted towards me. Most were still locked in conversation or trying to order a drink. I didn't expect all conversations to end straight away. Looking at the still dirty warriors, I didn't expect them to fall silent straight away.

After some thought, I opened with a song that might resonate with Hruk but also had a lively melody. More people fell silent as the riff picked up.

"Come on out of your cage. You're going to do just fine..."

Again, I took some liberty with the lyrics to make it more appropriate for the situation. I'd never played the song in public before. Liverpool clubs loved putting on Mr Brightside. Though I hated the environment, I did enjoy how everyone on the dancefloor would slow their movements to sing along. Samantha loved the song. So, I had learned it for her sake. Singing it now brought back memories of her.

Instead of images of her straddling someone else, I recalled the good times. Despite the pain she had inflicted me, I still remembered them fondly. I remembered the smiles and her fawning over my cooking. God, I missed the evenings with her listening to me play the guitar with a content look in her eyes. Then I realised those moments were gone forever. Not only because she'd cheated on me, but also due to my new reality. As sorrow replaced my previously almost-cheerful mood, my song selection started to reflect my state of mind.

The crowd didn't mind, though. Conversations fell silent, and eyes turned glassy. The more I sang, the more I craved comfort. I wanted intimacy to forget my troubles. That's when I spotted Lefa. Sure, my attraction to her was purely physical. It's not that I didn't like her, just her making fun of my naivety following the one-night-stand didn't sit well with me. I wanted her again. Sex not being a big deal to capper society made it a plus. Neither she nor anyone would expect a commitment from me; there couldn't have been a more perfect arrangement.

Lefa wandered over as I was in the middle of 'Wish You Were Here' by Pink Floyd. The song may have been too slow and sombre for the environment, but the crowd swayed along to it. Looking into the eyes of my audience, I realised the lyrics probably resonated with quite a few of them. Given the nature of their profession, the warriors must have lost several brothers in arms. They probably spent long periods away from home as well, missing their family and friends. Similarly, the civilians struggled with loss and separation too.

〚 **Musician Mastery has progressed to Journeyman: Rank 4**〛

I don't know what came over me, but as I neared the end of the song, I wanted to do something sweet. Asking Lefa to share a bed probably wouldn't be a big deal to most cappers, but on Earth, we never took such a direct approach. So, as I neared the song's end, I approached Lefa. While the final notes still hung in the air, I pulled the pink flower out of its temporary home on Gram's cloak and offered it to her.

Lefa's jaw dropped. Was gifting flowers to a girl not a thing in **Game World**? As far as I knew, most women loved such gestures. I had mixed feelings about them. I didn't see the romance in giving someone a dying plant, but that was probably me trying to sound cool and cynical. With a shaky hand, she accepted my gift and audible gasps spread throughout the room. I looked around confused. Did I do something wrong?

"By the spirits, Perry, yes!" Lefa exclaimed, throwing her arms around me, and my heart jumped into my throat. "I will marry you!"

"...What?"

The tavern burst into thunderous cheer and clapping. I spotted Hruk staring at me from not far away, wide-eyed.

"Seriously?" I wondered out loud remembering how the older woman and Hruk had spoken about the flower. They knew. The cappers didn't consider sex a big deal, but the exchange of a singular pink flower meant we were betrothed. "I was just trying to be romantic. I didn't mean to—"

"Of course! After those songs and the raw emotion behind them, how could I say no to you? To think you serenaded me all evening to build up to this moment. I couldn't have imagined something more perfect." She kissed me hard. Still in shock, I let her tongue part my lips and caress mine. The cheering intensified and people hooted as we kissed. Minutes ago, I would've appreciated her large breasts pressed against my chest—bloody hell, I would've gone for a squeeze while at it. Now I wanted nothing to do with them. Then, she pulled away. "I mean. That song didn't hold a candle to Wonderwall, but I couldn't have imagined a more romantic proposal in front of all my friends and family!"

My audience parted for Grog as he made his way over to us. The giant capper wrapped his arms around Lefa and me and lifted the both of us off the ground. "I should've guessed it when I saw the flower," he said, his face buried in our shoulders. "You were late because you wanted to make my daughter happy! I should never have doubted you, little man. My advisors said we should restrict your movement further, maybe even put a tail on you, but Lefa knew better." The Chief hiccupped as he rambled on. "She said you were a man of honour. I should've believed her."

"Da, are you crying?" Lefa asked, cutting him off.

There was no explaining the situation now, was there? If I told them the truth, I'd never escape the city.

"Of course I'm crying! My first daughter is finally getting married. I thought the day would never come." He put us down and wiped his eyes. "Perry, you're moving into our home immediately."

Heavens no! Forget the Champions of Pestilence. I didn't want to get tied down over something as simple as a flower. Someone should have warned me! More importantly, how could I commit to someone while memories of Samantha still had such a big hold on me? I needed to figure a way out quickly.

"That might not be the best idea," I said. Seeing the disappointment in Lefa's eyes hurt, but I didn't want to get forced into a marriage I didn't want. Sooner or later, Lefa would realise the truth and then things would get worse. "We jovians believe, betrothed individuals shouldn't spend the night together until after marriage."

"Fair enough, lad," Grog said. "Retaining one's culture is important."

"Besides, I wouldn't want to ditch Cook midweek." I couldn't tell whether **Facts Begin With Fiction** had come into play or not, but I intended to take full advantage of the trait's power. "Let me assist him until the wedding, or at least until he can find a replacement."

"We can respect that. Can't we Lefa?"

"Of course, Da." She nodded, beaming at me. "I like a man with principles."

I couldn't tell which made me more of a scumbag: ditching Lefa after proposing to her or considering Lily's plan of escape.

Chapter 16
Escape Plan

To put Lily's plan into action, I needed to overcome a major obstacle: stealing Gor's locket before he started his rounds. While the capper had enough Perception to escape my Charisma, he'd see through any attempt I made at snatching the resistance totem. I didn't have enough Control or the relevant Mastery. However, that didn't stop me from practising.

"I saw that!" Cook yelled. "You need to stop with these pranks, Perry." Rolling my eyes, I put the whisk back.

Some would say I was taking advantage of Cook's desperate need for assistance. People that have ever worked in a kitchen will know it's a game all cooks play with one another. It involves taking a tool or an ingredient another person needs and moving or hiding it.

"If you'd give me more to do than this boring busywork, I'll leave you alone, Cook," I told him. "I'm getting sick of peeling and chopping vegetables. Let me show you what I can do with meat."

"We need to stretch our meat," Cook replied. "If I let a prisoner have his way, we'll finish two weeks worth of meat in a day, and then we'll have riots again. I won't live through another one of those Perry. I just won't."

Cook had gotten very talkative over the past few days. Technically, I was no longer a prisoner, but he still referred to me as one. However, now that he would talk to me, I didn't mind as much.

"You've never experienced proper jovian cooking, have you, mate? We're country folk. When the cold months come, we don't have enough hunters to rely on. So, we try our best to stretch our ingredients as far as they go. Have I told you about my mother's winter cooking?" Cook put down his knife, moving his full attention to me. I knew he'd listen to a story if it involved food. It took more than a week, but now I could finally get him to listen to me. "I'm pretty sure I've told you this before, but my family used to run a tavern. So, no matter the weather, we needed some manner of meat on the menu or no one would order food. Given how amazing your cooking is, you must have worked with jovians before."

"I learnt everything I know from an old jovian in the Bracken Swamps," Cook told me. "He moved after marrying a wood aelph. The man wouldn't stop with his stories of jovian produce and livestock."

"So, you know how we like to use our ingredients. There were three things we'd never run low on. Potatoes, onions and mushrooms. So, come the winter months, mum would get all the bones the butcher intended on throwing away. She'd roast them and then deglaze the pan with red wine. We'd cook down dozens of onions in the pot and then throw in the meat and potatoes together for a low and slow cook. It'd be beautiful, I tell you, Cook, especially when we finished it with the mushrooms. Don't you want me to make something of the sort?"

"That sounds amazing, it does," Cook said with a dreamy looking in his eyes. Then he shook his head, refocusing. Damn it! Cooking Mastery and racial bonus together gave him too much Perception. "Why do you care, Perry? Another week and a half and you won't have to work in the kitchen with me. By the spirits, once you're married to Lefa, Chief could make you my boss! Are you Journeyman cook yet?"

"No," I answered.

"Well, I'm an Adept. If you ever get to Journeyman and want to come back and cook in my kitchen, I'll let you make whatever you want. I just can't risk my reputation on an Apprentice ranker's word."

> Congratulations!
> You have unlocked the Sleight of Hand Mastery.
> When you can't rely on your sneaky halfling ways, why not resort to distraction?
> Sleight of Hand Mastery has progressed to Novice: Rank 3!

So **Facts Begin With Fiction** had uses besides getting people to believe my stories. While distracted, he didn't see me move all his tools around. So, I could use the trait and my Charisma for misdirection as well. Bloody hell, even though physically I'd never achieve much in this tiny body, I could see the combination becoming very powerful. Now, I needed to do the same with Gor.

I tried over the following days but ended up getting a harsh reality check. I needed a lot more than a Novice ranked Mastery and a single-digit score in Control to remove a necklace from around the middle-aged cappers neck. Despite my stories, he found my attempts to chummy up and put an arm around his shoulders odd. No matter how hard I tried, I couldn't get to his locket. On the bright side, he didn't figure out my ploy.

So, I waited until his next day off until he gave me the locket willingly. Damaging the trinket wasn't an option. I needed it to ensure Lily wouldn't look for a loophole or trick her way out of the life debt.

As usual, Hruk and I took the food cart to the capper half of the prison together. I waited while he delivered the food. As usual, it didn't take him very long. Much to Hruk's surprise, I didn't take the cart another floor down to feed the remaining inmates.

"It's just two people," I told him. "Why don't we take the cart back to the kitchen and I'll go back with a couple of bowls? I don't see why Gor wastes his time pushing a cart around."

"I've asked him that question enough times," Hruk said.

The little capper celebrated the revelation. We now had one less floor to worry about. I needed to take my time and some privacy. Cook had already left for the day. He wouldn't miss me. Taking full advantage of my few remaining days of employment, he had left the kitchen cleaning to me. So, once he left me to my devices, I went straight to the cell housing the human prisoner.

"Hey, you," I whispered. "Come here." I didn't want Lily to hear our conversation.

The man flashed the same knowing smile as before. "I've been expecting you," he said. "The bones foretold your arrival."

"Please, spare me the speech. Did your bones tell you why I'm here talking to you right now?"

"That's not how divining works." His smile faded. "I saw a Champion arriving in Blacknail's Table and setting the city ablaze. I don't know how or why he'll do it, or even what it will look like, but when my divination works, it never lies."

"What makes you think I'm this champion?" I asked.

"After your conversation with the shadows on your first night here, I knew it had to be you," he answered.

"I'm not a champion, mate, but I've heard that the Champions of Pestilence are on their way here. I'm pretty sure chaos follows them wherever they go." The man stared at me, probably processing the information I had shared with him. Any other time, I would've pandered to his ego, but time was a luxury I didn't have. Even though Cook had gone home, Hruk could question my prolonged absence. So, I got straight to the point. "I'm staging a prison break. Are you happy in here or would you like to explore the possibility of getting out."

"What do you need from me?"

"If I got you the bones, could you create a replica of this?" I showed him Gor's locket. "You do that, and we'll take you with us when we break out of here."

"What then?" He asked. "You're going to burn this city of innocents down so you can escape?"

"Look at me, mate!"

"It's Sloane—"

"Don't you think if I had the power or *intention* to set the city ablaze, I would've done that already? Bloody hell, if I had any power at all, I wouldn't hang around here much longer." I sighed, regretting my volume. I wanted everything in place before sharing the plan with Lily. It was probably too late now. I could see her face pressed against the bars as she watched us. "I'm hoping we'll escape without any casualties. Can you help or not?"

"I guess letting the sexy aelf mind flay an innocent capper is the best way out." He took the locket from my hand and inspected it. "Shoddy craftsmanship," he commented. "Looks easy enough. I won't need my tools. Get me a handful of bones, and I'll Manipulate them into the same shape."

I had come prepared. To save on cost, Cook brought entire animals instead of butchered meat. He wouldn't teach me how to take them apart, but disposing of the bones was my responsibility. Sloane accepted the handful of bones hungrily. He picked through them, set aside three pieces and stuffed the rest into his pocket. The scrimshaw whispered strange words under his breath until the bones glowed a bright purple. They flew out of his hand and orbited an invisible point above his palm. I watched them speed up until they blurred, looking like a ring of purple.

When his spell ended a few minutes later, an almost exact replica of Gor's locket dropped into his palm. Sloane handed it back to me. I'd need to find a bit of twine and some colour to finish the look, but Gor would hopefully fall for the forgery.

"When do we get out?" Sloane asked me.

"Soon," I said, after taking a moment to find my words. Unlike Mind Magic, Sloane's methods had a more tangible effect. Though extraordinary, it wasn't enough to leave me speechless. "You'll know when I get your cell door open."

"Fair enough. It's not like I'm going anywhere." He sat down with his dinner and tucked into it. "Is there anything else I can help you with?"

"Yes. What manner of magic was that?"

"That's a very personal question to ask a stranger," Sloane replied. He ate a spoonful, looking me up and down. "Covenant. I made a Covenant with an entity that lets me shape, manipulate, and reinforce dead bone matter. Is that all?"

"For now? Yes."

Once done with him, I approached Lily. I showed her the mock totem and told her to get ready. We didn't have a plan for what we'd do after she escaped her cell but hoped the Mind Magic and Sloane's abilities would do the rest of the work. I still didn't like the thought of Lily turning Gor into a puppet, but what other option did I have? Sloane had foretold it, and the crypt troll had confirmed it: the Champions of Pestilence would soon set the city ablaze. The cappers didn't seem worried, but the thought had me terrified.

My betrothal to Lefa added to my urgency. As unattractive as I found cappers, race had very little to do with my unwillingness. Sure, I didn't like the thought of spending my life among a warrior based society. Lefa was beautiful, had perfect proportions and sweet. However, that wasn't a good enough reason for marriage.

After discussing our plans with Lily, I returned to the stairs. I found Hruk waiting for me at the top. He looked up at me with wide tear-filled eyes. "You're leaving?" Hruk asked.

"I'm sorry, mate," I said, placing a hand on his shoulder. "I know we've become great friends, but I can't stay here. Where I come from, proposals involve rings. I didn't realise a flower carries so much weight."

"That was no ordinary flower, Perry. You gave her a Heart Tulip! Why didn't you just speak up and say something? Lefa is an understanding woman. She'd understand jovian culture is different from ours."

"Do you really think so? I did it in front of all of her and Grog's friends. Bloody hell, even if Lefa is okay with it, I don't have it in me to disappoint Grog. Every time he smacks me on the back, it feels like my skeleton is going to jump free of my body." I understood where Hruk was coming from. Despite their unbelievably ridiculous customs, cappers had proven themselves sensible and understanding. To some extent, I was behaving like a coward and a douche. However, I worried, even if Grog didn't go full-on murderous-goblin warlord on me, he'd increase security or take away my freedom of movement. I needed the ability to move around freely to escape the city. "It doesn't matter, Hruk. I don't know how much you heard, but you can't tell them—"

"I won't," he said, interrupting me. "Perry, you've opened my eyes. I don't want to stay here anymore. My people don't care about me in the slightest. Maybe out there I'll find someone who has a fetish for short, skinny, green-skinned men."

"That's the spirit, mate. Perhaps we'll find your kink too."

Chapter 17

Escape from Blacknail's Table

The following morning I followed Gor when he set out to deliver his meals. Obsessing over the late vegetable delivery, Cook didn't care when I left the kitchen. Creeping through the shadows, I maintained a healthy distance from my mark. I felt horrible about what would happen to him. Some part of my consciousness hated me for facilitating it. I still had the real totem in my pocket. Gor hadn't bothered studying the necklace when I returned it to him. Though the shape matched the original perfectly, the colours weren't quite right.

"What're you doing here, Hruk?" Gor paused when passing the room where Warden stored the prisoners' belongings. As planned, Hruk had set himself there, waiting for us to escape. "Shouldn't ye be fixing the stairs in the lower basement?"

"I'll get to that later today, Jailor Gor," Hruk said, stuttering. The little capper and I made eye contact as I peeked at them from the shadows. "I just thought I'd clean around here first in case Warden does an inspection."

Okay. He deserved more credit than I had given him. It was a good enough lie. However, I worried his twitching eye and stiff posture would give Gor reason for concern.

"He's been threatening to do that for a while, hasn't he?" Gor laughed. "Just don't take too long, alright lad? My back is in bad enough shape already."

"Yes, Jailor Gor." Hruk nodded.

⌜ Sneaking has progressed to Novice: Rank 6 ⌝

My heart rate picked up as Gor finished delivering meals to the cappers. Watching the middle-aged capper struggle with the cart, I found myself tempted to help him. I wanted to tell him to leave the cart at the top of the stairs and just take two bowls down to Sloane and Lily. As lovely as Gor was, he didn't come across as the brightest of light bulbs—did **Game World** have electricity? Perhaps lanterns or torches would be more appropriate.

After several painful minutes, he reached the floor dedicated to foreign prisoners. "Damn floor," he grumbled when the wheel got caught in a crack. I clenched my fists as the wait became agonising. The capper kicked the cart free and trudged along, grumbling about his sore back. Even though Lily promised her magic wouldn't leave any permanent damage, I didn't believe her. I guessed the life debt wouldn't keep her from lying to me unless the falsehood had a chance of causing me harm.

Gor didn't pause in front of Lily's cell. Instead, he pushed straight past her towards Sloane.

"Wait!" she called after him, holding out her empty dinner bowl through the bars. "I'm hungry."

"What now, lass? Ye finally want to eat green-skinned cooking?"

"The jovian turned me."

"Ye leave that lad alone, ye hear?" Gor scolded, ladling our porridge for her. He passed it to her with an apple. My chest tightened as I waited for her Mind Magic to take effect. Gor didn't deserve this. "It's not like he's long for the prison anyway."

"Oh, you're setting him free?" Lily asked.

"The lad's marrying the chieftain's daughter," Gor answered.

"That's a shame! I like it better when he brings me my meals. It's a nice break from your ugly face."

"Aren't ye a sweet talker." The capper laughed. "Don't ye worry. I'll find a new helper sooner or later. You'll get someone new to play with."

"You better make him pretty, Mister Jailer. I don't want this someone new to be another capper."

The longer they spoke, the more friendly Gor's tone became. So, her Mind Magic needed some time to take effect. I recalled it hitting me almost instantly. Perhaps, the higher a target's Perception, the longer it took. I dared closer as Gor's body language relaxed. His eyes had a glassy sheen to them. When I saw him unlock Lily's cell without her prompting, I knew she had taken control.

"Open the human's cell, green-skin," Lily commanded. He obeyed. Neither of the two full-sized individuals could stand up straight in the corridor. "Lead the way and disable all the door wards, please."

"Yes, Inmate Dawnstar," Gor said.

"You may address me as Mistress. Come on now. Lets not dilly dally."

Gor didn't recognise me when I showed myself. Instead, he kept glancing between Lily and the way forward. It was almost as if we had never met. Leaving the food cart behind, we climbed up towards the prison's main floor. As discussed, we headed straight towards where Hruk was waiting for us.

Gor opened the door to the storage, and all the inmates rushed in. Sloane adorned himself in a long hooded coat. The scrimshaw squealed like a little girl when he got his hands on a long white staff. Etched runes and carvings of some strange four-legged creature covered it. It took me a moment to realise the tool was a solid length of polished bone. Sloane adorned himself with necklaces and hand-sized knives of the same material.

Not caring about our eyes on her, Lily stepped out of her clothes and pulled on a long charcoal dress. Everyone's eyes widened when the flash of exposed breasts came and went. She tightened it with a leather belt and then fastened a cape around her shoulders. She dug through the untidily piled weapons and came away with a long dagger and a cane. Lily strapped the former to her thigh and kept the latter in hand.

Hruk took the longest. I guessed the tiny capper had never worn fitting clothes. He tried on several sets of clothing and only settled on an outfit after Lily threatened to use her magic on him too.

"So, how do we get out of town?" I asked.

When Gor ignored me, Lily repeated the question to him.

"The front gate," he answered, the Scottish accent gone from his speech. Cosmic shit! What more could Mind Magic do? "The safest method of escape would be to stow away in an outbound cart. Since Chief started preparing for Lefa's wedding, more shipments have been arriving in town, and the guards have gotten lax with their inspections."

Gor and Hruk led us through the less-populated streets. Going unnoticed proved impossible. Our full-sized companions appeared human with their hoods up. However, even in the emptier streets, people recognised me. I guess high Charisma did have its downsides,

"It all starts with confidence," Lily told me. "As long as you don't give people any reason to worry, you can hide in plain sight."

So, I played along, greeting anyone who stopped to say hello or waved at me. Not letting concern affect my expression proved difficult when a warg rider waved at me. I almost tripped when returning the gesture. Fortunately, he didn't come any closer.

To avoid the shaman and his rambans, we stayed far from the market street and walked through residential areas instead. Unlike the rest of us, Hruk remained stiff and kept his eyes on the ground. No one paid him any attention. Wearing proper clothes, he blended in with the local populace more than anyone.

Besides my attention-grabbing cloak and still growing infamy, Sloane's staff drew the most attention. Due to their tribal heritage and the shaman led religion, Blacknail's Table obviously had a decent market for a scrimshaw's wares. However, I couldn't help but wonder whether the other communities of **Game World** had much demand for bone tools, weapons, or trinkets. More than one capper paused to admire the art etched into the polished length of white.

I sighed in relief when we finally reached the stables. So far, so good. Everything had gone according to plan. Now we needed to find carts to hide in. Unfortunately, all four of us couldn't fit into the same vehicle. So we split into pairs. Hruk and Sloane climbed into a cart of wine barrels together. It had enough room for them to lie down between the wooden casks. While the distracted merchant haggled with the stablemaster, we went over our plans again.

"A half a day's ride down the mountain, the road will split into two," Sloane said. "Disembark there and wait for us. We'll need to stick together to survive the wild's on foot."

"Understood." I shook hands with him. Hruk looked like he needed a little assurance, but before I could say anything more, the aelf returned. Lily and I scrambled to duck behind a bush, while Gor remained where he stood with a blank look on his face. "Lily, which cart looks like our best bet?"

She shushed me. "Let's wait until they're out first," Lily said, pointing at the warg riders chatting next to the gatehouse. Gor's information wasn't up to date. The frequency of inspections might have gone down, but they had canines to sniff out contraband and any unwanted individuals.

I held my breath as the wine merchant whipped his reins, guiding his horses towards the city exit. My heart leapt into my throat when he paused by the gatehouse. He lifted a small cask, no bigger than a human head, off his cart bed and threw it to one of the guards. They hooted in delight and waved him through.

"Great." Lily sighed. "Now which one looks comfortable enough for a long ride—"

She didn't get to complete her thought. I managed to pull Gor into the shadows just as Cook arrived, running. The chubby capper approached the guards panting and red-faced. I hoped the tubby man would collapse. He didn't. Instead, Cook spoke loud enough for everyone around the gate to hear. "Warden says to put the city into lockdown! There's been a prison break. The foreigners have taken Gor and the jovian hostage."

Cosmic damn it! The guards jumped into action. Half a dozen pushed the wooden doors closed together, ignoring the merchants voicing their displeasure. Catching his breath, Cook spoke to them in a hushed tone. Everyone around the gate had their ears strained, trying to eavesdrop. I guessed the capper authorities didn't want visitors and residents to find out their prison system had failed.

Lily grabbed my hand, and we ran into the narrow alley between tent-houses. Gor followed hot on our tails. We stayed close to the walls. Did Lily want to brave the wilderness on foot? I didn't fancy testing my speed against the wargs. Just as I thought of them, their howls sounded not far away. I hoped they'd take a few minutes to organise themselves before tracking us.

We weaved through private courtyards and people eating breakfast around communal fires. Too many people spotted us. Sooner or later, they'd alert the guards of our presence.

"Gor, is there another way out of the city?" Lily asked, coming to a stop after ten minutes. "As crappy as your walls are, I don't see any openings in them."

"We're not the best builders, Mistress, but us green-skins know how to put together a good defence," he said, beaming with pride. "That was the only safe way out."

"He keeps emphasising the word *safe*," I told Lily. "Ask him what other exits the city has."

"You heard him, Gor. Out with it."

"The tunnels, mistress," Gor replied. "I wouldn't recommend it. They're too dangerous, and no one's been in there for years."

"What about the other two?" I asked. "What if they're out there waiting for us?"

"They're on their own now," she answered, before turning her attention to Gor. "Take us there."

"But, mistress—" Gor winced, clutching his head. "Yes, Mistress. Whatever you want, Mistress."

"I wish you wouldn't do that," I commented. "He's one of the loveliest people I've met in this city. He doesn't deserve this."

"How about you leave that for when we're not being hunted, love. You're sweet, but there is a time and place for such sentiments." Her cold tone and display of power shut me up.

Chapter 18

Pursuit of Warginess

Lily tore a scrap of cloth from all our sleeves. Then, she pressed her hands together and closed her eyes.

"What is she doing?" I asked. The howls were closer now. The wargs were probably tracking our scents by now. "We need to move. They'll sniff us out in a second."

Gor smacked the back of my head and shushed me. "Don't interrupt the mistress!"

Where did he get off? I stopped myself mid-swing. No. Punching Gor would only earn me bruised knuckles and a terrible debuff. "I like you, Gor, but you do that again, and I won't stop your mistress when she attacks you again." The capper's green face paled on hearing my words.

When Lily opened her eyes, they glowed a deep purple. A similar light pulsed outwards from where she stood, feeling like a warm tingle as it washed over me. Then, Lily opened her eyes and smiled. Damn, that smile.

"So? What are we waiting for?" They'd be on us moment now. We needed to get moving already.

Lily pressed a finger to my lips. I couldn't tell whether it was her natural charm or if she'd mastered the process of using her sexuality as a weapon, but she sure knew how to get my blood boiling. Moments later, cats appeared out of the alleys, nooks, and crannies. Alley and house cats walked together in varying states of cleanliness.

Kneeling, she ripped the torn clothes into strips and tied them around the cat's necks, tails, and limbs. None of them hissed or scratched at Lily, but let her do as she pleased. Once done, she whispered to the felines, and off they went. Some disappeared into the alleys they had come from, others slipped through fist-sized holes in the walls.

"Now, they can't track us by smell. Clever, aren't I?"

didn't give her the acknowledgement she was looking for, while Gor stared up at her with adoring eyes. Finally, we got moving. Much to my annoyance, neither of my new companions displayed any sense of urgency. They walked at a leisurely pace as if there weren't wargs and cappers looking for us.

Gor took the lead, guiding us into the older parts of the city. Instead of tent clusters, we walked between poorly planned stone and wood buildings. More howls and barks sounded in the distance. The guards had probably rallied more wargs to their cause.

Were they out hunting for just Lily and Sloane? Cook did say they'd taken Gor and me, hostage. The question was: would Grog and Lefa believe that if we got captured. Grabbing Gor made sense, but what reason would they have to kidnap me? No. There was no backing out now. I had cast my die. Now we had no other option but to run.

All my time on Earth, I'd never had a panic attack. I grew up proud. None of my friends were as calm and collected as me. Then again, on Earth, I never had muscular, green-skinned men and their monstrous hyena-wolf hybrids chasing after me.

"Over there!" It was the scarred capper that had called me a pretty boy at Klinkle's. He spotted me through the ruins of an old stone structure. "Get 'em, boy!" he yelled, spurring his warg onwards. I recognised it as the friendly bow from outside Klinkle's tavern. Then again, I didn't have enough experience with the beasts to tell the difference. For all I knew, they all looked the same. Unlike the capper, the creature didn't need to go around the building. It had no trouble climbing over the crumbling walls and jumping from pillar to pillar.

"Run!" I yelled. My companions didn't need telling twice. They took off at break-neck speed, putting my nine points of Control to shame. So far, our leisurely pace had helped us avoid attention and suspicion, but now we overturned boxes and pushed strangers in our pursuer's way.

With every passing second, I fell further behind. Then, we turned too many corners to close together, and I was alone. I heard more barks nearby. The warg rider wasn't alone. I guessed the pursuing capper, probably the warg master, had called the rest of the pack. Hoping the nearby cats would throw off our scent, I kept running.

Though I didn't know where they went, I ran through open doors and jumped through whatever windows I saw. I had no hopes of outrunning the wargs. However, I could fit through places they couldn't, so I used that to my advantage. A couple of times, I felt hot, damp breathe on my shoulder, but I didn't dare look back. I couldn't afford a misstep or a stumble.

"Maka, *any* help will do!" I mumbled through ragged breaths.

No spider came to my aide. She had humoured me, after all. If we agreed to something profound, maybe the system would have highlighted it like Lily's life debt.

When I encountered a pie on a window sill, I grabbed it without thinking. No. I wasn't going to eat it. As much as I liked flaky pastry and what smelled like beef and stout stew, my current predicament didn't allow for snacking. Instead, when the pursuing warg got close again, I threw the pie over my shoulder. The sound of jaws snapping closed around it and chewing as the beast fell behind gave me some respite.

I recognised the locale. An expanse of tents lay to my right and the city's only architecturally sound area ahead. I guessed Grog lived there. Probably the shaman too. To my left stood a giant cliff face and the prison where everything started.

Then, I saw Gor again. His terrified head peeked out from behind a boulder along the cliff. He waved me over. Good. At least my blind running had taken me where I needed to go. Breathing heavily, I made my way over to him.

Lily didn't come across as the trustworthy type. Being under control, Gor didn't either. However, I didn't have any other options. They were my best and only method of escape. Unsure of Lily's agenda, I planned on losing them as soon as possible. Considering how she conducted herself, Grog's suspicions were likely correct. If she really was a spy, I didn't want to get caught up in any of her messes or end up like Gor. If I got the opportunity to break the lovely capper free of her control, I planned to take him by the hand and run, ditching Lily while doing so.

I was halfway there when a powerful force barrelled into me.

My mum never let me try rugby. She worried I'd never survive getting tackled. While that may have been false for my old form, it wasn't for my new one. I felt shaken to the core when my body rag-dolled into the cliff face. My ribs creaked, and the wind was knocked out of my lungs. I fell to the floor gasping for air, waiting to get mauled by an ugly maw.

The attack didn't come. Instead, I heard metal clatter to the ground next to me. Struggling to get my arms under me, I forced myself up. It was a pie tin. I looked up at the warg. Its saddle didn't have a rider. He must have fallen off when the canine went after the pie.

The monster licked my face before grinning at me, and I instantly recognised the goofy smile. It *was* the same creature I had met outside Klinkle's tavern. The warg licked me again, and despite the smell, I couldn't help but gasp out a ragged laugh. When I scratched him behind the ear, he showed the closed-eye look of ecstasy which confirmed he meant me no harm.

"You don't want to eat me then?" I asked. I looked past him and failed to spot Gor. The warg's eyes shifted between the pie plate and me. "I don't have any more pie."

When I picked up the dish, the creature's smile widened. It backed up, front paws tapping the ground. Oh. It wanted to play. Standing up straight, I threw the dish, putting my hips into it. The warg chased it like a dog chasing after a frisbee, and I ran to where I'd seen Gor.

Thankfully, he and Lily were still waiting for me behind the boulder. We entered the opening together before Gor slid a panel and the boulder moved to block the opening, plunging us into darkness.

"I was starting to worry you ditched me," I said.

"But you made it here nonetheless," Lily replied. She murmured a few words under her breath, and a trio of purple wisps blinked into existence. One stuck by her, while the other two drifted over to Gor and I. "I owe you a life debt, remember? Until you forgive it or the system decides I've done enough, you're safe."

"Lucky we ended up in the same place."

"No. When I cast the spell on the cats, I created a temporary psychic link between us. Even though you didn't know it, you were following me." Lily brushed her hair back and straightened her clothes. She didn't need to, but I enjoyed watching her move. "It's no different from whatever Mind Magic you used to calm the warg. I have to say, that was some quick spell casting. Your Mind and Control stats must be pretty damn high."

I didn't correct her. If she believed I had access to magic, maybe she'd stop trying to enchant me. I figured out Lily's plan. If she got me in the same state as Gor, she could just compel me to forgive her life debt.

"Gor, can the wargs follow us here?" I asked. "I don't think the cats will keep them distracted forever."

"No," he answered. "The tunnels aren't wide enough for them to fit and barely anyone knows about these tunnels. As far as I know, it's only me, the warden and a couple of retired jailors."

"Let's hope they spend all day searching the city and don't question Warden until tomorrow," I said. "What do you think, Gor? Do we have reason to worry?"

"Besides, even if they do find the tunnels. This place is a maze." Gor took the lead as we ventured deeper into the depths. It took me by surprise when he addressed me directly. "The Warden's late grandfather had the tunnels and path carved when the clan was at war with the Bracken kobolds. In case our walls fell, he and his family planned on escaping to Eldar's Plains. They don't like cappers down there, but it's better than dying slowly to kobold venom."

I missed my old body. I couldn't tell whether Gor's Control stat was just that high, or he had Masteries and perks helping him, but he easily scaled ledges and cleared crevices with no run-up. Though not as agile as him, Lily had longer legs and faced fewer challenges; at times she magically manipulated her clothing to wrap around rocks and pull her up.

Alright, maybe I didn't need offensive magic to survive after all. Lily's methods, though alarming, were effective.

I made up my mind. Even if I picked up Mind Magic—which I probably would since it scaled with Charisma—I wouldn't use it the same way as Lily did. The idea of invading someone's mind, and stealing their free will left me feeling slimy. I never wanted to become someone okay with anything of the sort.

All teenagers dreamt of discovering superpowers, but none of them pondered the ethics of it. I guess the line 'Who watches the Watchmen?' struck a nerve. I neither had Superman's sense of morality nor did I trust myself not to become Big Brother. There had to be other ways to put the School of Magic to good use.

"What are the limits of a life debt?" I asked Lily.

"I'm not your slave if that's what you're trying to figure out. I am open to getting into bed with you without being ordered to, but you don't own me."

"Why would you even go there?" Was she born a sociopath or had access to Mind Magic made her that way? "No. As beautiful as you are, I don't plan on taking you up on that offer. If we have a conversation and I ask you not to disclose what we discussed, will the life debt ensure you hold your tongue?"

"Only as long as the life debt lasts," she answered. "However, we can make a deal through the system for an exchange of information. You answer my questions, and I'll answer yours. Anything within the parameters of the deal will forever be for us to keep secret."

"And if one of us breaks the deal?"

"Permanent debuffs and the system arranges restitution to the wrong party. It could be a transfer of stats, a significant Mastery or property."

"Great, and this deal, once we declare the parameters, there is no going back?"

"No, the system won't let you."

⟦ **Lily Dawnstar has offered an Exchange of Information.** ⟧

⟦ **Would you like to add any clauses to it?** ⟧

I scrolled through the list until I found what I wanted.

〖 **Peregrin Kanooks has proposed Vows of Secrecy and Honesty.** 〗

Rolling her eyes, Lily agreed to it.

Chapter 19

The Three Best Friends That Anyone Could Ever Have

"Since you agreed to it, I guess you have questions for me too," I said. Lily nodded. "So, I'll let you establish the parameters first."

Gor took her hand as we walked and she pulled back in disgust. Though Lily had turned the capper into an enchanted thrall, she still looked at Gor like he was untouchable. Aelves really were the assholes of **Game World**. Gor deserved better. He'd always been nice to me.

"I want to know who you were talking to in the dungeons," she answered. "Admit you're a champion and tell me as much as you can about your patron."

⟦ **Parameters set.** ⟧

Perfect. I expected Lily to ask such questions. Keeping the subject secret would be difficult given the information I needed.

"I want you to explain how magic works in **Game World**, the different schools of magic and specifically your magical arsenal."

⟦ **Parameters set** ⟧

"I guess that confirms one thing. You're not of this world," she said, looking disappointed. I knew it! My ignorance of the world's magic betrayed my status as an outsider.

"I'm not. I'm a champion but don't have a deity."

"How does that work?"

"That's not a part of the deal," I answered, grinning. When no external force compelled me to elaborate, I knew I was in the right. "The Vow of Honesty confirms I'm not lying, but I don't have to tell you why I don't have a deity."

"Then who were you talking to?"

I told her as little about Boots and Maka as I could without showing all my cards. Lily's frustration was apparent. I knew very little. As a result, there wasn't much I could tell her. Still, I let her ask as many questions as she could, giving her minimal information while at it. It let her know, though new to the world, I wasn't some fool she could take advantage of.

Once she had exhausted her line of questioning, we moved onto my inquiries. Lily started off by listing the seven schools of magic: Creation, Shaping, Manipulation, Reinforcement, Mind, Life, and Covenant. Most of the schools were self-explanatory, but as she explained, the system tabulated the information for me.

Creation:
> Create something out of nothing. Though Mana hungry, the art of conjuration is powerful and much sought after.

Shaping:
> Mould the world in your image. Shift materials from solid to liquid without a change of temperature, or shape them however you please.

Manipulation:
> Control is power. Whether it be objects or the elements, with Mana, you may leash and Manipulate all using nothing but your will.

Reinforcement:
> Imbue and strengthen. Mana can empower the body, soul and the world around you.

Life:
> Heal and grow. Mana can give Life just as well as it takes. Whether it be fauna or flora, everything starts with Mana.

Mind:
> Not every answer lies in the physical world—telepathy, empathy, illusion crafting. When pushed, the Mind can do anything.

Covenant:
There is no shame in borrowing strength from another. Whether it be summoning or channelling a higher being's power, it all starts with making a Covenant.

Lily elaborated on **Game World**'s magic system. Being very Mana intensive, the first four schools demanded practitioners pick a focus. It made using magic more Mana efficient at the cost of limiting the range of spells available to the caster.

Once an individual learnt to sense Mana, they could seek out a place or being of power and earn a primary attunement. This attunement defined the basis of all their spells. With time they'd find a secondary attunement to add more applications to their primary.

The system informed me that Mind wasn't the only option. Covenant relied largely on Charisma too. I recalled Klinkle mentioning Bards getting Masteries like Beast Taming. I guessed it relied on Charisma too and would pair nicely with the Life Attunement. Mind was still by far the best candidate, but it was nice to have options. I could see myself casting illusions to distract and confuse foes while running away or directing my allies to attack them.

"Sloane told me he made a Covenant—"

"I heard what he said." She interrupted me. "It's probably some death-worshipping beast that gives him control over dead bone matter. He won't have the same power level as a Manipulator or Reinforcer focusing on bones, but some argue versatility makes up for it."

We were discussing the relationships between the different schools and how Mages combined their primary and secondary schools when we heard a distant scraping. It sounded like rocks grating against other rocks. At first, I tried to convince myself that it was the cave settling around us, but then the rhythm suggested differently.

Gor and Lily looked as concerned as I, and despite the low temperature, I found myself sweating. We didn't stop moving. There was nowhere to go but forward. Besides, if something did come for us, we had no option but to face it head-on. Lily's lights made us literal beacons in the darkness. Gor's racial night vision didn't work in the cave's complete blackness. So, we had no option but to rely on the little purple wisps.

Eventually, a crunch added to the scraping. It sounded like digging into a bowl of cereal when out of milk. Samantha used to call me a barbarian and lazy for not going out to the store. I didn't care. Corn flakes didn't need milk to be great. Damn it! I was going to die in this new world of magic and monsters without eating another bowl of honey-nut or maple-pecan-crunch.

"What is it?" I asked when Lily started murmuring under her breath.

"I can't tell," she answered, keeping her voice low. "The psychic feedback isn't giving me any useful information. It's something organic. I'm sure of that, but it's like reading a blank slate. Nothing is going on in there."

"It must be Little Linda," Gor said, calm as a cucumber. "She digs through rocks looking for creepy-crawlies and shrooms. Gran used to tell us stories about her. We don't know where she came from, but Little Linda is a friendly lass."

Lily nor I found his words reassuring. The sounds were getting much too loud. 'Little', worried me. What if it was an ironic use of the word? Like Little John from Robin Hood. The man was anything but little.

The rhythm made things worse. I imagined a troll much bigger than the one pushing the plague cart digging through rock with its nails and teeth. Maybe she fed on mushrooms and insects because she lacked better options. As lovely as the cappers were, their awful skin didn't make them look particularly appealing. Maybe Little Linda would feel differently about Lily and me. My trust in Gor dwindled as our journey continued. I couldn't tell whether it was all the stopping and starting whenever we reached a fork or the scraping and crunching were getting to me.

Then we found an underwater stream. Throwing good sense out the window, I dunked my head in the cold water. Things hadn't gone according to plan. Expecting ourselves at a rest stop after disembarking, we hadn't brought supplies with us. Anxious about the escape, I had only hydrated myself after getting out of bed. Now, after running from the wargs and spending several hours in the cave-system, my throat was parched.

"No dying until the life debt is repaid," she whispered, ruffling my hair. I couldn't tell whether she was doing it on purpose or not, but Gor and I struggled to look away when droplets splattered on her pale cleavage. At this rate, she'd wear me down by the end of the day.

The longer we walked, the less with it Gor appeared. He no longer resembled the cheerful jailor I had met in the dungeons. Drool dripped from the corner of his mouth, and his buggy eyes had long gone blank. It reconfirmed my worries regarding the power of Mind Magic. I wanted to ask her more about her magic, but keeping silent made more sense. Who knows what monster lurked beyond the field of our vision?

Further down the stream, we saw the first sign of life. We spotted a light dangling over the water. The yellow glow had a soothing air about it as if welcoming us to wander closer. When we got closer, we spotted more.

At first, I thought we had encountered some sort of bioluminescent vegetation. Then, a fish leapt out of the water, biting the tear-drop shaped light, proving me wrong. Glowing spikes sprang from the bulb, impaling the creature from the inside out. The line reeled itself up towards the ceiling, and we heard crunching echoing down.

"What manner of creature is that?" I asked.

"I don't know," Lily said when Gor didn't respond. In his dazed state, I didn't expect an answer from him. "If these caves are locked off from the rest of the world, there might be creatures that have adapted to the local environment and Mana specifically."

"So, the gods and Cosmics don't create everything then?"

Lily didn't answer my question. I guessed religion was as complex a subject on **Game World** as it was on Earth. I thought with there being evidence of higher beings, there'd be fewer debates regarding the matter. Also, it reminded me not to make assumptions. As opinionated as Lily appeared, she likely had beliefs of her own. Understanding the magic system wasn't enough. I still had a lot to learn about **Game World**.

Our lights had halved in size. Lily's shoulders drooped, and her eyes appeared somewhat glassy. I guessed keeping Gor placated and maintaining the purple wisps had a drained her Mana.

I got nervous when we saw giant glowing mushrooms in the distance. They stood as tall as Lily and light filtered through the veins beneath the mushroom caps. On spotting them, intelligence returned to Gor's eyes. Lily's control over him was waning. He ran over to them and scrambled up the shortest of the lot. Following some heaving and groaning, the capper managed to pull the cap free of the stem and returned to Lily holding it out as an offering. Good. Though not in full control he remained enchanted with Lily.

"Mana oyster mushrooms, mistress," he grinned. "They pack a punch but will keep you going for days!"

Lily and I looked at each other with hesitation in our eyes, but her expression changed as soon as she sniffed at the mushroom's gooey contents. Gor peeled back the veins revealing fluorescent orange and purple jelly. The aroma wafting off it carried earthy notes with a touch of fruitiness. My rumbling stomach urged me to consider the nourishment.

Gor took the lead. He scooped a handful into his mouth and the cheery intelligence he had first displayed when we met, returned to his face. "The shamans use it to help them commune with the spirits," he explained.

While the comment made me hesitant, Lily tested the substance with her index finger and licked at it. Her eyes widened at the taste, and she dug in. Was it just Mana the mushrooms provided or did they have psychedelic effects too? I had no issues with hallucinogenic or relaxing substances. Bloody hell, when my family dug through my freezer on Earth, they'd find two blocks of Cannabutter, but there was a time and a place for everything.

Lily visibly relaxed as she ate and Gor appeared more in control of himself. Despite their insistence, I refused to partake. Tripping out in a cave with monsters wasn't my idea of a good time. The tantalising aroma called to me. It wanted me to taste, but I refused to give in. Lily sat down holding the mushroom cap and ran her hands down her cheek, neck and down to her breasts, leaving a trail of glowing jelly behind. Her eyes flared purple, and all of a sudden, my body demanded I join her and consume the material as well.

"Go on, laddie," Gor insisted. His old Scottish accent had returned. "Yer gonna need the energy once we're out of the caves."

"I'm fine thanks, mate," I said, trying my best to maintain a cheery tone. However, the now crazed look in Gor's eyes made my voice waver. Lily didn't say anything. She continued to eat the jelly, covering herself in it slowly, sensually. Much to my surprise, she didn't recoil in disgust when Gor ran a finger up her breast scraping a line of jelly off her skin. He licked it off his fingertip and grinned. "Doesn't look like my kind of thing."

Grabbing a handful, Gor advanced on me. "I swear ye'll like it, lad. Come on, don't make me force ya."

Chapter 20

Mushroom Dodging

I could tell from Gor's face. He wasn't playing around. In the ambient light, he finally resembled the fantasy goblins I had grown up with. He lunged at me, one hand outstretched to grab and the other ready to stuff luminescent jelly down my throat. What the hell was going on? How did he go from his placid self to this aggressive brute in seconds? It had to be the mushrooms.

Fortunately, though they didn't affect him as much as they did Lily, Gor wasn't in top form. I had little trouble side-stepping the very telegraphed lunge.

"What's going on, Gor?" I asked in a half-horse stance. I was born premature and spent all my pre-adult years short and skinny. So, mum enrolled me in Shotokan Karate. The Pacifist trait had rendered most of it useless now. However, the footwork came in handy when dodging the next lunge. "C'mon, mate. You don't want you to do this. We're friends, aren't we?"

"Yer not my friend." He laughed. "Ye want the mistress, and yer not having her. She's mine, I tell ya!"

"Don't you see what's happened, mate? It's Lily's Mind Magic! This isn't you." Keeping eye contact, I slowly backed away, trying to find flat ground. I'd have an easier time dodging him without any obstacles getting in my way.

His second attack was too close for comfort. The footwork would only get me so far without technique. Gor's knobbly shoulder grazed mine, throwing me off balance. My old block-and-counter instincts threatened to kick in, and I fought to reign them back. I wasn't sure whether it would count as engaging in combat or not, but I couldn't risk it.

I needed to run. Maybe if I put enough distance between Gor and me, he'd give up. Then, I'd follow the stream or whatever markers I came across until the exit appeared. After that, I'd use the six silvers in my pocket to find a way to Eldar's Port. I could put this whole episode behind me. It's then I remembered I had forgotten to collect my tips from Klinkle's. Now wasn't the time for such concerns, and I cursed myself for thinking about money.

On second thought, no. My conscience would never let me get away with it. If I escaped, I'd be leaving Lily in Gor's grubby hands. As much as I disliked the aelf, I could imagine what fate the capper had planned for her. He'd likely keep her on a diet of mushroom jelly and have his way with her repeatedly. No one deserves such a fate.

So, when I did get the opportunity to run, I sprinted into the little forest of mana oyster mushrooms. It wasn't far enough for Gor to give up the chase. Once I was sure, he had lost sight of me among the stalks, I fell into a crouch and focused on slowing my breathing.

"You hiding from me, laddie?" Fortunately, Gor's Perception wasn't enough for him to spot me straight away. "I promise I won't do anything too bad."

His boots scraped the stone floor, giving away his location. So, Sneaking Mastery wasn't a part of his repertoire. Or, that's what he wanted me to think. No. I wasn't going to let myself get complacent. Why was he so keen on feeding me the damned mushroom jelly? Was this some 'Invasion of the Body Snatchers' bullshit? Wouldn't killing me make for a more sensible option? Considering my Brawn stat, he likely only needed a punch or two to put me down.

Magic and friends. That's what I needed. As much as I wanted to focus all my resources on Charisma, it wasn't going to be enough. Hell, even something along the lines of trap making would go a long way. I didn't have a relevant mastery or the tools, but something along the same lines would prove invaluable when escaping wargs and hopped up cappers.

My giant, bare feet helped me keep quiet as I crept around the mushrooms. Fortunately, Gor's Perception wasn't enough to track me. I guessed the capper had focused all his stats in Brawn and Control.

⟦ Sneaking Mastery has advanced to Novice: Rank 8 ⟧

I needed a plan of attack. Sneaking around wasn't a permanent option. So, I followed Gor. I still couldn't figure out what was going on with him. Had he snapped under Lily's Mind Magic? I guessed her spells stemmed from awakening a target's carnal desires. Maybe, with Gor, she had pushed it too far. Or, had Lily subconsciously projected her view of cappers on him, and now Gor was emulating what she expected; I couldn't be sure.

A plan began to form. Despite the air of malice about him, Gor wasn't in full control. He was under the mushroom jelly's psychedelic effects too. Of course. The shamans used it for communing with spirits. It had some significance in capper religion. I assumed they, as a species, had a much higher tolerance of the substance. However, if I managed to force enough on him, maybe I could get him in the same state as Lily.

Once Gor was far enough from where I hid, I targeted the shortest mushroom with the widest cap. My Brawn wasn't sufficient to break it off as quickly as Gor had, but after several minutes of rocking the cap back and forth, I managed to get it free. The sweet, earthy aroma assaulted me as soon as I removed the veins and the urge to dig in returned with a vengeance. Samantha often complained I was too stubborn; for once, it did me a world of good. Maybe willpower was a more appropriate term, but it wasn't the time for semantics.

"C'mon, laddie, I've got a sweet lass to enjoy," Gor called. "It's no fun if she passes out altogether before I get to her. Why don't you come on out? We'll share some of this lovely treat, have a chat, and then everything will be okay."

Armed with the heavy mushroom cap, I approached him. Gor stood on a rocky outcropping above the stream. The several hanging angler bulbs behind him made it difficult to focus on his features. I could only see his crooked silhouette.

"Fine," I said, making myself visible. "I'm not going to beat you, so why not join you?" His tense shoulders relaxed when he saw the full mushroom cap in my hands. "Let's sit down together, share some of this jelly and talk things out."

"Finally, ye come to yer sense." He laughed. "I was starting to worry ye were going to run for the exit. Ye could've ye know, lad? We're so close." Gor looked at where the stream disappeared into the wall. I couldn't see a way out of the caves or more tunnels, but he was right. I could feel a light breeze blowing towards us.

"I'm not going to make it out there on my own. You know that mate. I considered running at first, but then I realised you don't want to kill me." I pointed at the chunk of wobbling jelly still clutched in his left hand.

"Of course not, I want to offer you to Little Linda." The swaying lights cast their glow on Gor's grinning face. His yellowed teeth and manic eyes sent shivers running down my spine. I knew it then. He was no longer the capper I had befriended. "The stories say, she likes her prey live and docile. I reasoned if she and I can strike up a deal, I'd not only get to keep the sweet aelf lass for myself but also make a worthwhile Covenant. You have no idea how hard it has been for us practitioners when the shamans hog all the clan's spirits."

"So what? You want to go back to Blacknail's Table with an aelven woman on your arm, and a summon to show off to your friends?"

"Ye read my mind, laddy," he said. "Now go on. Eat the jelly. Make it less painful for yerself."

"How about we sit together and share it?"

"What do you take me for? A fool?" Gor laughed.

"Not at all," I answered. "But, how depressing is a final supper if you go at it alone. An experienced jailor as you should know. Don't you think so, mate? Come on, share it with me. You obviously have the constitution to bear it. I'll be out of it long before you start getting loopy." Gor stared at me long and hard, unsure whether to trust me or now. "C'mon, it's not like I can beat you in a fight anyway and Lily isn't going anywhere. Humour my last request, please?"

"Fine." He waved me over.

I marched forward with all the confidence I could muster. Once, I was close enough, I feigned tripping on a rock and flung the goop at his face. Okay, no debuff yet. Much to my disappointment, he blocked most of it with his arm. Of course, his higher Control stat made his reaction time much quicker than mine.

Shooting me a wicked grin, he scooped a fresh handful off the ground and rushed at me. I was out of options. The only way out was to backpedal, and Gor would have little trouble catching me. On either side was the sharp drop into the stream below, so I reacted on impulse and summoned Diya. As soon as the guitar manifested in my hands, I used it to block Gor's fistful of jelly. Fortunately, it didn't trigger the Pacifist trait's debuff either.

Roaring like a mad beast, Gor swiped at me with his free hand and barely missed. I teetered on the outcropping's edge, struggling to regain my balance. I didn't know how jovians fared with swimming, but on Earth, I'd never been particularly good at it. Then, the capper grabbed me by the throat, and there was nothing left to stop his large hand from shoving the luminescent jelly down my throat.

Screw reigning in impulses. It was time to do or die. I swung Diya up between his legs, and he yelped as all air rushed out of his lungs. A heartbeat later, a wave of weakness washed over me.

⟦ **You have violated the Pacifist Trait's commandment. All stats have been halved until you get a full night of undisturbed sleep.** ⟧

Fortunately, I didn't need my halved Brawn or Control. Gor stumbled backwards, and mustering the last of my strength, I pushed him into the curtain of dangling bulbs. Trying to regain balance, he fumbled about, and managed to wrap his hands around the two in front of his face. Spikes sprang from them, biting through his hands. Gor screamed loud enough to alert everything sleeping within the caves.

"Help!" he shouted as the anglers started pulling him up, looking at me with desperation in his eyes. As much as I wanted to, I couldn't. My half point of Brawn could barely carry my own weight. My knees turned to jelly, and I collapsed in a heap. It felt like someone had struck me in the back of the head even though there was no pain. Or, maybe I had fallen out of the stupid tree and hit every branch on the way down.

Gor's struggling body disappeared into the darkness above. Crunches punctuated his screams until everything went quiet. Despite my halved Perception, I caught a glimpse of the creatures above. They reminded me of rock lobsters. Stone covered shell, several legs, ugly spines, and antennae that ended in large luminous teardrops. My chest tightened thinking of the pain Gor must have felt. None of this was his fault. Lily was the one that had pushed his mind to the point of snapping, but I had let her do it to escape Blacknail's Table. Now, I would have to live with the consequences of my actions.

I tried standing up, but my body had forgotten its motor skills and the concept of balance. Struggling on my hands and knees, I crawled through the mushroom forest. The fog clouding my mind made it difficult to remember which direction we had come from. Fortunately, my Perception of four was enough to spot Lily's jelly slathered form propped up against a rock. I did a quick check of my stats.

⌈ **Identification:**
    First Name: Peregrin   **Last Name:** Kanooks
    Race: Jovian   **Patron:**—
    Health: Poor   **Mana Core:** Full

Stats:
    Brawn: 0.5⇩   **Control:** 4 ⇩
    Mind: 1.5 ⇩   **Arcana:** 0.5 ⇩
    Charisma: 7.5 ⇩   **Perception:** 4 ⇩

Traits:
    Pacifist
    Fact Begins With Fiction
    Arcane Chords

⌋

    If the debuff wasn't bad enough, I now lacked the willpower to fight exhaustion. It added to my struggles as I dragged myself back towards Lily. Maybe once she came to, she could keep watch while I got some sleep. Huh. I guess I finally earned the life debt.

    I reached Lily after what felt like hours, covered in sweat and fighting nausea. My consciousness was fading fast, so I gave her a good shake. Lily didn't respond. I checked her pulse. Good. The jelly hadn't killed her. I needed to rest my head. It weighed as much as my body. No longer thinking clearly, I lay it on her stomach and struggled to stay conscious. However, Lily's warm and soft body was much too comfortable. Despite my halved Perception, I tried spotting the angler ceiling lobsters. Instead, I ended up counting their luminescent bulbs, and it lulled me into a deep sleep.

Chapter 21

Fresh Air

I didn't feel as poorly when I woke up. My stomach still complained from not having eaten in who knows how long. However, my stats had returned to normal. Lily smiled down at me from her upright position as my head lay on her lap.

"I didn't mean to fall asleep," I said, too comfortable to get up. She stroked my hair, and I enjoyed the feel of her soft fingers on my scalp. "At least we're okay."

Lily's soft breast grazed my face, and I didn't mind. It wasn't so bad. Hell, we were both consenting adults: would it be so bad if I gave into my urges? My Charisma and the locket together were enough to resist Lily's Mind Magic. I'd ensure she didn't enchant me. Screw it, after what we'd been through. We could both use some intimacy.

Sitting up, I pulled Lily in for a kiss. She leant in without any resistance. Damn. I'd never tasted lips so sweet. They parted as I slipped my tongue in, my left hand pressed against her stomach before sliding up to gently caress her right breast. Damn.

Lily felt good. Despite my hunger and thirst, my trousers tightened as I touched her. Why was I holding myself back until now? Lily's nipple hardened at my touch. Eager to taste it, I ended the kiss. Then, getting a better look at her, I stopped. Something wasn't right.

The only light around us came from the mushrooms, angler crabs and the jelly still in the cap at our feet. Lily's wisps weren't around us. Now that I was sitting up, I could see her eyes clearly. I didn't see any life in them. In fact, while my hands explored her body, Lily's arms hung inert at her sides.

Alarmed, I pulled away from her. Even though she responded to my kiss, Lily was in no state to give consent. What the hell? Did I just molest her? Holy shit! I almost had my way with her!

"Lily, are you okay?" I asked, grabbing her shoulders. I gave her a good shake, but she didn't respond. Lily continued to look at me with the same placid gaze, her smile not fading. "What the hell is going on? Is it the jelly? Magic backlash?"

My old gaming knowledge was useless in the situation. I didn't know what to do. Lily didn't fight me when I forced her eyelids open to study her pupils. Opening her mouth, I checked her tongue. No different. Well, the jelly had stained it purple, but besides that, it appeared normal.

I lifted Lily's left arm above her head. When I left it there, she didn't lower it. The limb remained in its position even after I moved away from her. I didn't like this one bit. Slapping Lily wasn't an option, I couldn't afford the debuff again. We'd gotten lucky. I didn't know what the system considered a full night's sleep, but it had to be at least six hours. We'd survived in an unknown cave full of strange beasts without getting attacked; we weren't going to get that lucky again. Besides, I needed to get Lily some help.

Okay. We needed to get out and as far from the caves as possible. I hoped Grog and his wargs weren't waiting for us beyond the exit. Standing up, I urged Lily onto her feet. She followed my instructions like a merry infant. Taking her hand, I led her down the stream.

I saw movement in the mushroom forest. Its illumination had faded since I last saw it. For the first time since waking up, I noticed the constant crunching and grating had stopped. It wasn't the time to give in to curiosity, but I dared a peek. I was right. Little Linda wasn't little after all. A worm as thick as a tree trunk sat feasting on the mushroom caps.

Despite my better judgement, we edged closed to the mushrooms. I needed to have a better look. Gor wanted to make a Covenant with the entity. The worm rose out of the stone floor through a very snug hole.

Around it, lay grey sludge. Melted stone? I couldn't be sure. I should've tried learning more about the creature from Gor. If it truly had some incredible power, I could use some of that.

I'd have to come back for it. For now, I needed to get Lily and me to safety. And, some food in my belly. With some coaxing, I pulled her away from the terrifying sight of Little Linda—unless that wasn't her but a baby. No matter how much I tried, Lily refused to pick up the pace. If I pulled too hard, she'd dig her heels in and refused to continue. After several painful minutes, I managed to get the zombie-like aelf to where the stream disappeared into the cave wall.

"Where now?" I wondered out loud. We stood around where Gor had been looking. Still, I couldn't see an exit. Letting go of Lily's hand, I pressed both of mine against the cave wall. I didn't know what I was looking for, but pressing an ear against the cold, damp surface didn't tell me anything either.

I couldn't find a secret lever or a panel anywhere; what was I missing? I focused on the soft breeze. What direction was it coming from? Above? That didn't help in the slightest. I couldn't see any surfaces to climb up or any external light to follow.

When I opened my eyes, Lily was no longer by my side. She'd taken advantage of my distracted state and started running. I preferred her when she appeared catatonic. Now, it felt like getting a new puppy.

"Slow down!" I yelled, chasing after her. It's not that she was running exceptionally fast. The issue was her legs were much longer than mine, and my last meal was two sleep sessions ago.

Then she went around a large boulder and disappeared. Of course. When I got there, she was waiting for me at the mouth of a long tunnel, and I could see daylight in the distance. I guessed her height had helped her see something I'd missed. Maybe she wasn't completely useless after all.

We had to be extra slow during our descent due to the steep downward incline. Fortunately, we reached our destination without incident. For once **Game World** had decided to give me a break. We exited through a rocky hillock with a tall mountain behind us. I guessed Blacknail's Table was somewhere far above. Looking ahead, we saw a large expanse of flat, green grasslands. Eldar's Plains, I assumed. Best of all, below us, beyond a small thicket of trees, I saw civilisation.

"Good job, Lily," I said, taking her hand and giving it a light squeeze. I didn't trust her not to run off once again. The aelf didn't pull away. I waited for her to reciprocate my gesture, but she didn't. "It's alright. I'll get you sorted as soon as possible." Since she didn't understand a word I said, I took the opportunity to vent. "If you were any more of a bitch, I would have ditched you. Gor didn't deserve any of that. I don't know what you did to him, but that wasn't the capper I knew. There should've been a better way."

Airing my grievances to Lily in her helpless state didn't help. I'd never been one to say 'told you so'. We pushed onwards. Hopefully, things would soon get better. That's right. Trying to be optimistic, I studied what lay ahead.

The town appeared much smaller than Blacknail's Table. Unlike the capper city, its stone walls appeared to be of sound construction. It had a wide walkway for guards to patrol along the top of the ramparts, and several watchtowers for them to keep an eye on the horizon. Come to think of it. The settlement looked more like a fort than a town.

I guessed Blacknail's Table didn't need such a defence system due to its location on top of a plateau. From the way Klinkle described it, the city only had one road leading up to the gates. The steep cliffs ensured an opposing force couldn't sneak up on them, or for attackers to establish siegeworks. I assumed like the city's residents, opposing forces that meant them harm didn't know about the cave system either. The cappers hadn't wronged me. So I had no intention to expose the opening in their defence.

Instead, I analysed the settlement. One and two-storeyed wooden buildings dotted the space around the walls. I spotted patches of green with sturdier buildings bordering them. In the town's centre stood a sizeable cone-shaped building. With each floor carved into a massive step, it looked like several giant circles stacked on top of one another. Patches of green grew along those floors giving the construction a lush appearance one would expect of a fantasy world. A massive pillar stood at the top, reaching for the sky like an antenna. For a while, I wondered whether the settlement's residents were friend or foe. Then I realised my only other option was venturing into the wild.

"I reckon we're more likely to survive if we can reason with whoever attacks us," I said. "What do you reckon, Lily?"

Lily didn't respond. Instead, she watched the horizon with a blank look in her eyes.

"Good, we're on the same page."

Once again, I had to drag Lily behind me. She was no longer the woman I had met before. As we walked the serpentine path downhill, I theorised what had happened. With my very limited knowledge of the magic system, there were high chances my hypothesis was wrong. Gor said that the capper shamans used the Mana Oyster Mushrooms to help them commune with spirits. What if they did this through astral projection? Maybe Lily got stuck outside her body, or she suffered some sort of shock trying to get back in. It's likely I was wrong. However, it helped me deal with the strangeness of my new reality.

Now, that we weren't in any immediate danger, I wondered: what happened to Hruk and Sloane? Thinking about them, helped me push thoughts of Gor's demise out of my head. I'd never forget the look on his face when the lanterns got him. Just thinking about it made my stomach churn. For a moment, I was sure I saw the old Gor in the moments before he got pulled up into the shadows. Did he feel betrayed?

No. I'd be better off thinking Lily had broken him. If I didn't push him, he'd overpower me and feed me to Little Linda. Because of what I did, Lily wouldn't have to spend the rest of her days as a brainless sex slave.

More focused on leaving town, I hadn't thought about what would happen at our destination. Sloane said we wouldn't survive the wilderness unless we stuck together, but Lily claimed the fork had a rest stop. Couldn't we have arranged for transport once there?

Hruk wouldn't have left Blacknail's Table if not for what I had said. It had to be more than finding someone who'd find him attractive. Sex and love were great motivators, of course, but I believed we'd become friends. The capper looked like he'd never had friends before. Hruk's people treated him like an outsider, but I didn't.

I hoped Sloane would treat the capper well. Sloane and I didn't get the time to get familiar with one another. He did come across as a standup guy though. I didn't expect him to take care of Hruk indefinitely, but I hoped Sloane would get him to safety. I didn't know how the capper would manage. Considering how Lily spoke to Gor, I imagined the more 'advanced' races didn't treat goblinoids well. However, Hruk did have a useful skill. Maybe someone desperate enough for a Scribe would hire him.

Chapter 22
Lily and Hyacinth

"Ho, there!" The guards called when we approached the gates. "State your business, friend!"

"Capper raiders attacked our caravan," I called. "My friend here is injured. We're in need of assistance."

After spending time in Blacknail's Table, I felt bad vilifying the cappers. However, during my time in the city, I learnt that Grog and his warband hungered for battle. When they couldn't find a beast to take down, the chieftain would lead his riders to attack passing traders not allied with his city. It made sense using the bit of information to my advantage.

Up close, I realised the settlement was better defended than I assumed. A wide moat surrounded the walls and without the drawbridge lowered, reaching the gate would prove impossible. I assumed they had another exit on the side facing Eldar's Plains.

"It's not every day we see an aelf and jovian together," an older member of the guard said from across the moat. "Your lack of luggage doesn't instil confidence either, boyo."

"We had to abandon everything when the cappers attacked. I told the caravan leader, getting this close to Blacknail's Table was a bad idea, but he wanted to save time and labour cost." I hoped the humans didn't have enough Perception to overcome the effects of **Facts Begin With Fiction**. "Didn't do him much good though. The asshole cheaped out on guards too. Most of them ran when the raiders came."

Lily tried to pull her hand free. Looking at her eyes, I could tell she wanted to go swimming at the moat. Unwilling to let her go off in her current state, I tightened my grip.

"You don't have to let me in," I told them. "I can try to make it to Eldar's Port on my own. My friend, though—the cappers fed her something. She's not herself right now. Let her in and maybe take her to an apothecary, a medicine woman or whatever you have in there."

The guards huddled together and spoke in hushed tones. I hoped my bluff worked. The guards probably knew a jovian would never make it all the way to the port city on his own. After several agonising moments, the oldest guard opened a door by the gates and disappeared into the settlement. Not long after, we heard the mechanisms within the walls move and the drawbridge lowered to create a path across.

"Don't try anything," the guard warned when I led Lily across. He turned to his colleagues. "Take them to Lady Hyacinth. She'll want a word."

As soon as we passed the gates, the number of uniformed and armoured individuals took me by surprise. Some patrolled the streets while others stood casually around the shops and eateries.

Lily drew a lot of attention. The dried mushroom jelly had coloured her skin purple and orange. That, combined with her revealing clothes, reminded me of the girls from music festivals on Earth. Ah, I'd miss those scantily-clad lovelies. They were a wonderful bunch.

The open spaces had men and women running drills with their weapons, and the number of blacksmiths took me by surprise. Our guide explained, Hunter's Watch housed a military garrison. Even though the human-run settlements of Eldar's Plains were at peace with the Bracken Swamps and Blacknail's Table, despite the occasional caravan raid, their relationship had always been tense. Hunter's Watch served as the first line of defence ensuring no military force entered the plains.

As it turned out, they hadn't used the mountain-drawbridge in close to a decade. Lily and I had taken them by surprise. No one approached the settlement from the mountains. The councils assumed the cappers, kobolds and other denizens of the Wild Lands killed all members of the caravan or took them prisoner. No reputable merchant ever travelled close to capper territory. They either took airships or went around the swamps and sailed down the river.

Good thing **Facts Begin with Fiction** had done its job. He gave me plenty of information regarding the workings of the settlement and on how to proceed. I regaled him with a thrilling tale of how we fled our pursuers despite Lily's near-catatonic state and how a crazed capper had tried to feed me to a beast and take her as a sex slave. The man warmed up to me, the more we spoke.

Up close, the settlement's central structure proved a lot more impressive than before. I saw shops on the individual layers, stables and soldiers sparring. My previous assumption turned out to be correct. The build was some sort of fort. The man led us into the structure and to an elevator. I didn't expect to encounter such a contraption in **Game World,** It took me by surprise. We went up several levels, straight into a large circular office.

Armoured individuals stood guard around the entrance and thoroughly checked Lily and me. Once they were done, Lady Hyacinth finally graced us with her presence.

"What have you done to her?" the woman asked as soon as she saw Lily. Lady Hyacinth immediately checked the aelf's eyes, tongue and pulse.

"He claims capper raiders fed her mana oyster mushrooms, ma'am," the guard captain explained. "The hounds had a little sniff and went crazy. Don't think they were lying ma'am."

"What a shame, she's such a lovely girl." Lady Hyacinth tutted. "Who is she to you?"

"No one," I answered. "I just couldn't leave her behind. Didn't feel right."

She stared long and hard as she sized me up. I couldn't tell whether Lady Hyacinth believed me or not. I couldn't disclose we were on the run.

What if whatever treaty they had in place encouraged the extradition of prisoners?

"You did a good thing, boy," she finally said before turning to the guard. "Make sure he's cleaned, fed and clothed. As lovely as they are, I always thought jovians were cowards. But, you did a good, brave thing. I commend you for it."

> By impressing an individual of power or good reputation, you have earned a commendation.
>
> You may keep it to increase your renown in their settlement or redeem it for a favour.
>
> The nature of the favour may change how the individual views you.

"Thank you," I said. The concept intrigued me. I had never encountered such a concept in any game I had played on Earth. I found it odd she handed it out without question or investigating my claims of a capper raid. "For the record, we're not cowards. Jovians do the right thing whenever we can; just never at the cost of self-preservation."

"And a spine too?" Lady Hyacinth laughed. She clicked her fingers, and the guards guided Lily into a side room. I followed. "Well, I guess I had your kind wrong. You have my apologies, Master Jovian."

Keeping the commendation held no value. I already knew what kind of favour I needed to ask for. However, I didn't want the woman to think I was ditching Lily straight after getting to safety. Hell, I'd already ditched Lefa when she expected me to marry her. As much as I wanted to deny it, that made me an asshole. Now, I needed to give Lily at least one night before leaving.

"What's wrong with her?" I asked. Lily had become obsessed with the healer woman's curly hair. She'd pull on her wavy locks until they were straight, and then let them bounce back into their curls. "I haven't known her for long, but usually she's a lot more put together."

"The symptoms of mana overload differ, largely depending on an individual's attunement. I take it she's a Mind Mage?"

I nodded as my stomach sang the song of its people. Pressing a hand on my belly did nothing to quieten it.

"Mushroom jelly in its unrefined form is toxic," she continued. "Cappers have grown a tolerance for it over the centuries, but aelfs, not so much. Due to the race's arcanic inclinations and dependency, it's like catnip to them. So, when she indulged, your pretty friend let her Mana run wild, and it damaged her psyche. Whatever enchantment she tried to use on your attackers backfired." Lady Hyacinth sighed, brushing a strand of hair out of Lily's face. "Enough of that depressing talk, go rest."

The guards tried to usher me out of the room, but when I struggled, the woman shooed them away. Grumbling, the guard captain stepped out the door and stood facing away from us. We waited for him to close the door, but he didn't.

"Is it permanent? We just met yesterday, but I don't feel right leaving her while she's like this."

"Why? Do you have somewhere to go?" The woman tilted her head to the side, studying me. It was then her hair fell to the side, revealing her aelf-like ears. The rest of her features didn't match Lily's, but I guessed they came in all shapes and sizes. Maybe a racial variant? I realised at that moment, besides ensuring Lily's safety, the woman was trying to figure out whether I meant her kind any ill will or not.

"I'm trying to get to Eldar's Port," I said. "Hoping to get some bard and Arcane training."

"Interesting," she said. "Jovians with a thirst for adventure are truly rare, and everyone likes a good bard. I don't know whether there's any work in town for someone like you, Mister—"

"Kanooks. It's Peregrin Kanooks, but I prefer Perry."

"I'm Hyacinth," she told me, flashing a lovely smile. "You've done a valuable service to my kind, saving one of our own. I'll ask around whether there's anyone in need of a hand. It's Market Day today. Come nightfall, the farmers will be heading to their homesteads, and many of them do business in Eldar's Port too. I'll see if any of them are in need of an extra pair of hands for a week or two. Do you have any farming relevant Masteries?"

"No," I answered honestly. Since Hyacinth was upfront with me, I thought it best to reciprocate the gesture. "I've dedicated my life to music. I have Sneaking and Mana Sense too, but I don't know whether they'll be any use on the farm."

"That's certainly not going to make things any easier, but I'll see what I can do."

Things were moving awfully fast. I expected she'd want me around for a few days at least as she studied Lily's condition. Or was it the opposite? Maybe, Hyacinth's intention was to get rid of me as soon as possible. Either way, I chose not to look a gift horse in the mouth. The further I got from Lefa and Grog, the better.

"Thank you, Hyacinth."

"Go clean up, Perry," she said. "I've got work to do."

Chapter 23
On the Road Again

I felt good in my new clothes. Off-white shirt, black suspenders, dark brown trousers, and a matching coat. They were all children's clothes as the settlement didn't house any citizens my size, but I didn't mind. They didn't chafe, and that made me happy. Hyacinth's people offered a new cape as well, but I rather liked Gram's ugly gift. It made me feel like a glorious patchwork hobo.

Wary about surprising my new employer, I summoned Diya before our meeting time and slung the guitar over my shoulder. I had considered redeeming my commendation and getting an ensured job opportunity out of Hyacinth but then decided against it. For someone looking to build a future on their Charisma, commendations, renown, and reputation would all come in handy. Instead, I hoped the meeting she had arranged would end on a positive note.

Hyacinth and I headed to the bottom level of the fort, and a trio of guards walked us towards the gate facing Eldar's Plains. We passed a market full of men, women, and children not in military clothing. I guessed they needed civilians to run a settlement too. Soldiers would occasionally want food not prepared by their barrack's cook and have a drink away from their commanding officer. The people wore simple clothing and appeared hard at work, but they looked happy. Living in a military-run settlement probably let them enjoy a degree of security most couldn't find in **Game World**.

Towards the end of the street, sat the stables where we'd be meeting my new employer. He arrived at the stables as soon as the clock struck seven: exactly a quarter-of-an-hour after us. I could tell from the look on his face, the man prided himself on punctuality. Hyacinth introduced him as Walter. The human had a thick ginger beard, bald head, and was built like an ox. Looking at his stern face, I knew straight away, he'd be a hard man to please.

Walter looked me up and down before turning his attention to the guitar. "How good are you with that?" he asked. A giant hairy goat as tall as my shoulder wandered in while we spoke. It butted its head against Walter, and he swatted the beast away.

"I'm a Journeyman," I answered.

"That'll do."

"You don't need someone with Beast Taming?"

"No. My livestock are harder to tame than wolves." The goat was looking at me now. Its thumb-sized horns looked like stubs when compared to the rest of his body. "Most of the herd are nannies, and they're the friendly sort. They keep to themselves and do what their leading billie tells them. The males like this fine billie goat can be more of a challenge." He pointed at the creature now approaching me with curious eyes and a collar hanging around its neck. "Though effective, the enchantments cause them too much pain. So, we use music to keep them docile."

"I can do that," I said, looking at the goat nervously as it wandered closer. "I hope Hyacinth told you. I'm only looking for something until I can afford passage into Eldar's Port."

"That works just fine," Walter told me. "My boy is the house musician, and he's down with a cold. You'll be helping Samuel with taking the herd out to graze until he can play his flute again. Besides, he's constantly falling asleep in the fields and letting the herd wander. Maybe you can keep him in check." Walter's body language relaxed as we conversed. He probably put on his initial stern demeanour to intimidate me. After dealing with Grog, his put on airs didn't scare me in any way. "Next month, I have a delivery to make in Eldar's Port, and I'll drop you off. You'll have food and a board, but the job won't pay a whole lot."

"I was expecting to lose money getting there. So, even if it's a little bit, that'll be enough." I smiled, reaching out to pet the goat. It took a step back, moving out of my reach. "What you're offering is too good to be true. I mean, it sounds like you have everything you need. Are you sure I won't just be another mouth to feed?"

"I owe Lady Hyacinth a favour, boy. That is all." I knew it. She was trying to get rid of me, after all. This felt awfully fast. It felt too much like a trap, but I needed to keep moving. The sooner I found my place in my new world, the better. "Besides, the farm can always use an extra pair of hands."

Then, things started falling into place. If Lily really was a spy, then there had to be an intelligence network relaying information back to whatever power she served. What if Hyacinth was a part of the network? Maybe, she wanted me gone, so the authorities had fewer people to question. That had to be it. Hyacinth thought of me as a tool Lily had picked for her cover, and now she needed to get rid of me.

I had dozens of questions bubbling inside of me, but I thought it best to keep it to myself. The cappers had some sort of summit coming up, and Hunter's Watch sat as the first line of defence against a rival nation. The commendation, calling in a favour: Hyacinth wanted me happy and far away. It explained her rush.

"You don't owe me anything," the aelf said, clasping the burly man's hand. "This lovely young jovian risked his neck, bringing one of my people to safety. He's got a good heart, and I'd like to see his ambitions fulfilled."

Wow. Hyacinth liked to lay it on thick. I grinned ear to ear, playing along. If she knew I suspected Lily of spying in Blacknail's Table, I'd be too much of a liability.

"Well, Eldar's Port needs more people like you, Perry," Walter said. "Unless someone gets the Merchant's Guild under control, we farming folk are in for a hard time." He shifted his gaze to the goat. "Looks like Curry has already taken a liking to you, Perry. Maybe you'll do just fine."

Studying Hyacinth, I had almost forgotten about the goat. It hopped forward and headbutted me. The move felt more playful than hostile. However, I wasn't as stable as Walter, and the force knocked me onto my bottom.

"Yep, I think you'll do just fine." He laughed, helping me up. We discussed the job opportunity a while longer. It felt too much like charity, but for someone in my position, turning the offer down would be a bad idea. On the bright side, maybe I'd pick up a useful Mastery while I was at it.

Hyacinth let me bid Lily goodbye. It didn't matter, the aelf didn't recognise me. We stood alone in the healer woman's herb garden as Lily watered the plants. I couldn't tell whether she understood what she was doing or not. In fact, when I spoke to her, she didn't so much as look at me. I hadn't developed any sort of emotional bond with her. However, after what we experienced escaping the wargs and then surviving the tunnels, to some extent, we had become companions. It may have only been for a day, but to me, it was a first.

I considered forgiving the Life Debt. It no longer mattered. Besides, I wasn't sure whether I wanted Lily ever to find me after she recovered. Then, I decided against it. If she really was a spy, maybe someday I'd find myself in need of her services. Besides, if she ever did track me down and I didn't have the stolen locket or Life Debt for protection, she could turn me into a puppet too.

"Hyacinth, can I ask a favour of you without using the commendation?" I asked before leaving the garden.

"Depends on the nature of the favour."

"I made a few friends in the caravan. A man and a capper. They're very recognisable. The man is a bone carver and carries a unique scrimshawed staff. The latter is a scribe—"

"A capper scribe?" Hyacinth interrupted. "Are you sure about that."

"That's what he claims, I've never seen him practising his trade." In all honesty, I didn't know what kind of job a scribe did. "You'll know him when you see him. Hruk is an adult, but he's shorter and skinnier than any full-grown capper, has charcoal hair, and smooth skin."

"If they come through here, can you please let them know I'm heading towards Eldar's Port?"

"Sure," she answered. "You didn't tell me the man's name."

"Sloane."

"Consider it done." Hyacinth and I shook hands. "I'll pass it on to the watch. No need to redeem the commendation for something so simple."

Dusk had just settled in when we set out on Walter's cart. A pair of horses pulled it while the giant goat trailed behind us. For the first time since coming to **Game World**, I could be at ease. Things were falling into place. Sure, I had no idea what I'd do after reaching Eldar's Port, but for the time being, I had no immediate concerns.

Hunter's Watch would hopefully keep our pursuers at bay, Lily was in safe hands, and Hyacinth had her eyes open for Hruk. For the time being, there wasn't much else I could do. Continuing to beat myself up about Gor or worrying about Hruk wouldn't do me any good. Peregrin Kanooks needed to take care of himself.

Walter's goat wouldn't take his eyes off me. Occasionally, it would flare its nostrils and jerk its head upwards, as if issuing a challenge. What did the hairy monster want? I sure hoped he was an anomaly.

"He's a strange kid," Walter said when he noticed our staring contest. "His brothers sold straight away, but not him. Even with the control collar, I can't get him to stop headbutting people."

"That's a kid?!" I exclaimed, eyeing the goat. He was almost as big as a warg. "He's huge."

"Believe it or not, Curry is the runt of his family." Walter laughed at my wide-eyed surprise. "His sisters are already bigger than him. I've tried selling him to a rare animal merchant, to the butchers, and tailors, but no luck. They'll buy my butter and cheese, but Nil Mountain Goat is too exotic for their dinner table and too wild for anything else."

Walking up to the edge of the cart, the goat headbutted my leg—this time, harder than before. When I tried to pet it, the creature shied away again. What did it want?

"You'll see more of his siblings when we get to the farm," he continued. "I plan to sell the rest in the city. They're more open-minded in their selections of meat and fabric."

I'd never been a fan of goat meat. Maybe in **Game World**, it would taste different, but on Earth, the gamey smell always put me off. Walter told me about his family business. They kept a half a dozen billie goats for mating purposes. The diverse genetic pool did well to prevent too much inbreeding between the stock. The rest of the flock were female. He made a living selling their fur and milk. A while after birthing season, he'd cull the male kids not ideal for breeding.

"What does the collar do?" I asked, studying the device around Curry's neck.

"If the wearer does anything against their master's wishes, it causes growing pain until they obey," Walter explained. "I can't tell whether this one has a high tolerance for pain or gets off on it. He doesn't respond and keeps doing the same thing over and over again. Maybe he's stupid."

"I think he's just stubborn," I said. "That challenging stare in his eyes is pretty familiar."

"Whatever it is, I hope he sells soon. I'm not sure where he puts it, but Curry eats as much as his brothers."

"That's a sick name, you know," I said, amused. "Born to end up in the pot?"

"It's morbid, I know. My son thought of it."

When Curry came in to headbutt me again, I tapped his head with my giant bare foot. He hopped back, his big goat mouth, hanging open. The goat appeared slighted. I didn't want to risk him putting more strength into his next attempt, so I quickly swung Diya onto my lap and strummed a tune. I started with one of my own songs. After the incident with Lefa, I decided not to test Wonderwall's power again.

For a while, the beast stared at me with a sceptical look in his beady eyes. In my opinion, Curry deserved more credit. Walter knew more about the species than I, but I thought I saw intelligence in him. Or, it could be the opposite. Maybe Curry *was* just stupid and I was jumping to conclusions. Perhaps he didn't realise the collar hurt him whenever he misbehaved.

I was halfway into the song when Curry sighed a very goaty sigh and continued following us with a more relaxed expression. Now that I understood the world's magic system, I recognised the Mana's flowing through the guitar and me. As expected, the smaller pool of green energy coming from the guitar carried the Life Attunement. I still failed to recognise the second Mana's nature. Maybe it had no attunement at all. Lily did say people sought out places and beings of power to give their Mana a type.

Walter became more talkative when I finished my song. I guessed when talk failed to exercise my Charisma, Music did the job. I checked my Mastery Menu. Of the ten slots in the Active tab, six were full.

⌈

Cooking Apprentice: Rank 6
Dodging Novice: Rank 3*
Mana Wielding Novice: Rank 2*
　　-Mana Sense Novice: Rank 4*
Musician Journeyman: Rank 4
Sleight of Hand Novice: Rank 3*
Sneaking Novice: Rank 7*

⌋

That's right, I had a new Mastery. I earned the Dodging Mastery when showing off my fancy footwork. I'd been more concerned about clearing my vision to deal with Gor, so I had swiped the notification out of my sight and forgotten about it.

All but Musician Mastery had experienced some degree of growth. I guessed levelling them at Novice rank took a lot less effort as well. The rank hadn't budged since I finished playing Wonderwall. True, I didn't recall how long I had played Diya after meeting Lefa, but I remembered flashes of her sitting upfront while I played a few more songs.

Now that I had my freedom, it was time to plan out how to fill my Mastery slots. Planning builds, and theorycrafting had always been one of my favourite parts of playing games. Now, I would need to do the same for my new reality. Over the past few weeks, I had realised Charisma alone wouldn't get me anywhere. I still intended to dump all my free points in Charisma, but I needed Masteries that would pump up my other stats.

For the sake of survival, I needed Perception and Control. I expected all my current Masteries besides Mana Wielding to add to them. I'd need Mind and Arcana once I got an Attunement, but I had no idea how long I would have to wait before finding an entity or place of power. After suffering the Pacifist Trait's debuff, I understood the importance of investing in the other stats. Again, we got lucky in the caves.

"You don't have any Weapon Masteries?" Walter asked when I listed the contents of my screen. "I know your kind aren't keen on fighting, but surely, you learnt something to defend yourself."

"I never had to until now," I told him. "We as a people, stick together or surround ourselves with friends that can do all the fighting for us. Weapons training detracts time for the more fun things in life."

"Yes, yes, you don't have to tell me about jovian ethics. I hired an older man of your kind to help on the farm for a season. As soon as the sun dipped beyond the horizon, he would disappear to nurse his ale. You're not one of those jovians, are you?"

"You don't have to worry. I barely drink."

"Not what I heard," he mumbled.

I tried catching Walter's eye, but he turned his attention to the darkening road ahead and didn't look back at me again. Did he know something I didn't? I recalled several full-blooded humans drinking in Klinkle's caverns. Maybe Walter heard rumours and pieced things together. Or, Hyacinth knew more than she claimed. It didn't matter either way. Blacknail's Table and Hunter's Watch were now behind me.

I did feel bad for Lefa; none of this was her fault. We just came from different cultures. Though the impending threat of invading champions worried me, I'd be lying if I didn't admit: they were merely an excuse. I was the asshole here. How the hell was I supposed to know the Heart Lily—Tulip, whatever, signified proposal. Bloody hell, after making it clear that she didn't want a relationship after our night together, why did she even say yes?

At the end of the day, I could justify the matter however I wanted, but my conscience would likely need a lot more time to excuse my actions.

CHAPTER 24

A MEETING OF DEITIES

We encountered several checkpoints along the road which connected straight to the capital No wonder Walter laughed off my concerns of bandits and thieves. However, given the distance between the military installations, I worried armed men and women were ready for us among the bushes. On second thought, that was paranoia born of my initial impressions of **Game World**.

A near-endless expansion of tall grass surrounded us, occasionally punctuated by wild-canopied trees and farms. I imagined hiding amongst it wouldn't be an easy feat. Whenever we crested a hill, I'd spot woodlands in the distance. I guessed the more dangerous creatures that I expected of Game World limited themselves to the darker corners. The frequent patrols we saw likely kept adventurous predators at bay.

It was well past midnight before we stopped for the night. Someone had trimmed down the grass to create a circular clearing by the road. A log cabin sat far to the side serving food and drinks to people seated on the tables placed outside. The horses and other pack animals stood tied by a long trough on the opposite side of the clearing. And a bonfire burned in the centre with several carts parked around it.

Walter tied the horses with the other the beasts of burden while keeping Curry isolated in a far corner.

"His kind like to pick fights," he said. I could guess why. Like me, most organisms didn't enjoy getting headbutted over and over again.

After my long day, I was ready to pass out as soon as we took a seat by the fire. If Walter didn't offer to share the picnic he bought at Hunter's Watch, I probably would've. I didn't mind partaking in the meal. He claimed she always packed extra and it did look like three portions.

According to Walter, we'd reach our destination by evening the next day, so we didn't have to worry about rationing.

Looking behind us, I could no longer see Hunter's Watch, but the mountains it kept an eye on were still visible. Blacknail's Table would be on the other side. I guessed Grog and his people would have caught on to Lily's cat trick by now. Maybe they were sending riders into the wilderness looking for us. I hoped the military garrison did its job and kept the oversized capper from coming after me. The wargs could likely blend into the grasslands perfectly; their riders would stick out above the tall grass like sore thumbs. Hopefully, the patrols would probably get them before they got as far as us into Eldar's Plains.

According to Walter, it was close to midnight. It felt like a lot later given the distance we had covered. To be fair, the road barely had any traffic and was well maintained, so nothing had slowed or obstructed our journey so far.

The plains weren't as cold as the plateau I'd left behind so I only needed Gram's cape to keep me warm as we went to bed. The small roll of spare clothes Hyacinth had provided served as a decent pillow.

I dreamt of the massive tree again. This time, I didn't just feel the strange presences but could see them straight away. Front and centre stood a woman that reminded me of my mother—middle-aged, arms crossed, and brow wrinkled from constant frowning. Though she stood barely taller than me, the woman carried a gigantic and powerful aura. I knew instantly that my charm wouldn't get me anywhere with her.

A younger woman stood to her left. She looked a lot like a wood aelph—minus the cheeriness. Unlike the first woman, her skin was smooth: no wrinkles, crows feet, or laughter lines.

Behind them in the shadows lurked a third unfamiliar presence, and Maka sat on the tree trunk above. This time, her spider form had taken on a more colourful display. Instead of a hairy, brown tarantula, her new body had more slender features. I didn't know how, but I knew it was her straight away.

"I was just telling my friends, Perry," she said. "You're an individual worth noticing."

"Where were you?" I asked, not caring that the individuals present were likely gods or deities. "We had an agreement! You were supposed to help me until I was out of Blacknail's Table and safe. I almost died back there!"

"But you didn't die, did you?" I couldn't be sure where Maka's solid-black eyes were looking, but I could feel them boring through my very existence. "Besides, you left the agreement open-ended. Unlike in your homeworld, safety is an almost nonexistent concept here. Your best chance at safety would start with finding a patron, which I've been working at tirelessly. You should be thankful."

"That sounds like excuses and a whole lot of bullshit," said the presence in the shadows.

"You're one to talk!" Maka exclaimed. "Lord of Shadows. Your entire existence is based around deceit, assassination, and thievery. I'm not sure I can stomach getting told off by you." she returned her attention to me. "Like the Cosmics, our influence in the world of mortals is limited. No one can act outside their domain or in the absence of a conduit. It's not that I didn't want to help you, Perry. I couldn't."

"Excuses," the older woman said. "Always with the excuses. I swear, you young ones never own up to mistakes."

"Excuse me, Demi, I believe spiders and story-telling came long before anyone on **Game World** started harvesting crops." Maka's retort set the woman off scowling. "Shadow and I are *much* older than you. Just because you choose to look like a wise old woman, it doesn't mean you are one."

"At least I'm still remembered and worshipped, Maka." I could feel her fury raging within like a rushing flood threatening to wash us all away.

"Only the worst of the worst follow Shadow. While you. Nobody remembers you. Not even bedtime stories mention you now, Maka."

"Now that's just hurtful." Maka's tone suggested otherwise. "I know we've had our differences, Demi, but let's forget that for now and focus on why we have assembled. None of you has Champions at this time, and you all have aspirations to ascend. You need Outworlder blood for someone to carry the title, and we have that right here."

"Hold on a second," I interrupted, taking a step back. It didn't make a difference. We were in a dreamscape. I could retreat however much I wanted, but there'd be no getting away from them. "You need my blood? I'm not willing to ally with anyone that needs my blood. My blood stays on the inside, alright?"

"Calm down, Perry." Even though her eyes didn't move, I was sure Maka just rolled them at me. "I didn't mean it in the literal sense."

"God-like entities talking about blood gives me a reason to worry. My planet's history is full of communities practising ritual sacrifice to appease their gods."

"Maybe that's not the worse idea," Demi said, with a slight day-dreamy gaze. "I'll need to talk to my acolyte about that."

"How about we focus on what matters?" Maka brought the conversation back on track. "Demi, jovians are your favourite folk. What do you say? Perry could be a great candidate."

"Do you have any interest in farming?" She asked me.

"No," I answered.

"Then, we won't work out. My champion would need to work the land. All my gifts would revolve around improving his yield and defending his territory. As a deity of harvest and floods, there is little I can offer him."

"What about you, Hershey?" Maka turned her attention to the younger female deity. Throughout the exchange the aelph had stood still, studying me. "Perry here just risked his life saving a beautiful aelf girl from a horned up capper. He could have easily run to safety and left her behind. That's the kind of champion you'd want."

"He also proposed to a capper woman and then ran for the hills," Hershey replied, her eyes had a pink glow about them as she studied me. "No. Someone that's okay with doing anything of the kind won't do. Besides, my gifts of scorn and spurned advances are designed for women, not men."

"Then why did you bother answering my call?" For the first time ever, I sensed Maka's irritation.

"I've waited quite a while for the chance to turn you down, Maka." Hershey lips spread into a thin, tight line. I guessed that's as big as her smile got.

"Yeah, everyone knows what you're like," the spider retorted.

"What's that supposed to mean?"

Having already moved onto the final attendee of the meeting, Maka ignored Hershey. "What about you, oh great Lord of Shadows? He is little and sneaky; surely, you can use him."

"I thought I could until I met him," Lord of Shadows said.

"Oh, he's just young and new. I'm sure if you try hard enough, you could turn him into an excellent thief."

"It's not that, Maka." The mass of darkness shifted, resembling a cloud of smoke more than a person. "You failed to disclose his Pacifist Trait. Perry is a magnificent candidate, but I can't have a champion incapable of getting his hands dirty."

"I can get my hands dirty," I said. Given the power emanating off my current company, I had lost my voice for a while. However, thinking about how good a match Lord of Shadows and I would be, I forced myself to find it. "I killed the capper. If necessary, I'm willing to pay the price of going against the Pacifist trait."

"I can tell, child." The cloud of smoke rippled and I could see a person within it. "You have great potential, and we'd be a great match. I'll reconsider my stand if you ever shed the Pacifist Trait. Unfortunately, I just can't afford to invest in you until then. Even if you swear off banditry and assassination, thievery and espionage often demand the spilling of blood. I can't have you disabled and weak like you were in the cave. Your opponent was weak and crazed. Luck is a fickle mistress. Next time she may favour your opponent instead."

The cloud dispersed, Lord of Shadow's presence faded, Demi's body exploded into dandelion fluff which floated away, and Hershey simply walked off into the woods.

"Well, that could've gone better," Maka said.

"This feels pointless. I'm sure you knew none of them would want to back me." The pressure exerted by their presence had faded, but the experience left me spent and gritting my teeth. "Are you scraping the bottom of the barrel? Hershey, the Deity of Scorn and Spurned Advances? What makes you think she and I would be a good match."

"Watch your tone, Perry," Maka's jovial tone turned icy. "Do not forget, to me, you're no more than a fly. Meeting a deity in any form is an honour. Thanks to me, you have now met four. You're not exactly champion material. So, the candidates are those desperate or bored enough to answer my calls."

"I'm sorry," I said, realising my error. Maka was right. Given her status and the help she had already provided, she deserved my respect.

"Besides, the point of this exercise was to get you noticed," she continued, sounding friendly once again. "They might be lesser gods and a far cry from the Cosmics other champions serve. But, they are beings of power at the end of the day. They can still grant you blessings, make the rewards of an achievement favourable, or provide assistance if you amuse them."

When I woke up the following morning, we were already on the road. Since I'd fallen asleep in the back of the cart, Walter didn't bother waking me. I got to admire the beautiful countryside, but nothing of interest occurred during the remainder of the trip.

We stopped at a small town for the night. Walter picked an inexpensive inn. He covered the cost of the room, but I paid for my meals. In the morning, he tried selling Curry again, but by noon when no one showed any interest, so we continued our trip.

I could no longer see the mountains behind us. The thought of Grog being beyond the horizon put my mind at ease. I played my guitar to pass the time and much to my disappointment the Mastery didn't see any growth. However, since I kept it active at all times, Mana Sense gained a rank.

As sunset approached, I noticed the grass surrounding us was considerably shorter than it was when we started our trip. Farms became a more common sight and often appeared in small clusters. We reached Walter's home at nightfall, and after dinner, we went straight to bed.

.

CHAPTER 25

A GOATHERD'S LIFE FOR ME

We started our day early on the farm. Walter's son, Samuel, and I let the goats out of their enclosure into a large fenced field. They ran off to stretch their legs while we cleaned the barn.

Growing up, Mum joked if I didn't get over my wild fantasies and focused on academics, I'd end up working the fryer at some fast food joint. I never understood what the big deal was. I loved french fries, chips, and everything else of the matter. Maybe a kebab shop that did chips with cheese and gravy would work better.

I wondered how Mum would react if she saw me shovelling shit now. No. She deserved more credit than that. Mum wouldn't put me down. She'd give me a big hug, a kiss on the forehead and tell me everything would be okay. Mum would assure me that there was nothing wrong with shovelling shit. All manner of work had value. If it didn't make me happy, sooner or later I'd find a way to pursue something I liked. Mum would tell me she believed in me. The thought of never seeing her again made my chest tighten up; never having another mouthful of chips with cheese and gravy hurt almost as much.

Once we finished piling the goat shit into carts, we refilled the barn's troughs from the nearby well. The non-stop work had me sweating bullets and soaked my clothes through. Unused to manual labour, my knees wanted to collapse in on themselves. My shoulders and waist weren't far behind. I imagined it'd be much worse if not for my massive jovian feet's support.

After finishing the morning chores, I sat on the fence eating a breakfast roll filled with scrambled eggs and bacon. It reminded me of home. Every morning on my way to classes, I'd grab such a sandwich from my local cafe; fortunately, **Game World** already had one of my favourites. To help forget the homesickness, I focused my attention on the goats.

The females had long, sleek necks and narrow frames. They stuck together, watching their offspring. The youngest of the kids was my height. They bleated and played chasing one another.

I spotted six goats with almost no neck, giant heads, and chipped horns. Given their distinctly bulkier bodies and bigger size, I guessed they were the males. The billies kept their distance from one another. In contrast, the kids of Curry's age hung out together, charging one another with their stubby horns. Despite my position on the far side of the field, I'd hear their skulls thunking on collision. I guessed that's how the adults chipped their horns.

Curry stood in a far corner watching the kids play. He stood at two-thirds the height of the other males. Occasionally he'd approach one of the others and headbutt them lightly the same way he did me, but they'd ignore him. The kid reminded me of Hruk. Both struggled fitting in due to their status as the runt. The capper's issues were probably more nuanced, but I still couldn't help but draw parallels.

"He's too small," Samuel said, riding upon a horse. He wiped at his running nose, sniffing hard to clear his nostrils. "Da doesn't give them enough credit. They're not stupid. The kids understand Curry is too small to partake in their charging games."

"Poor guy." I sighed. I remembered being the third shortest in the year and among the skinniest. My classmates would often leave me out of their games.

"Do you know how to ride?" It was then I noticed the much smaller animal behind him. The boar had similar dimensions to Curry but packed a lot more muscle. Both the horse and boar had a short pike strapped to their saddles, and Samuel had a bow slung over his shoulder. "Don came to us from a hobgrem rider. We got her for mum, but since she passed, he's mostly been helping us forage for truffles."

"I've ridden before, but I remember being bad at it," I answered honestly. "If you're asking whether I have the Mastery or not, that would be a no."

"Well, it's time you learn," Samuel said, wiping his nose. "Happier the goat, better the meat and milk. Every day we take the goats out on the hills for a few hours. That's where I need your help. We don't like using the collars unless necessary, and as you can tell, I'm in no shape to play my flute."

As soon as I got off the fence, a strong push knocked me down onto my hands and knees. Of course. It was Curry. Rejected by his own kind, he had snuck up on me. Though I felt bad for him, the regular headbutts were getting on my nerves. If he didn't stop, I'd risk the Pacifist Trait's debuff and strike back.

Unlike the Nil Mountain Goats, Don proved a much friendlier beast. While the goats shied away whenever I tried to pet them, the boar accepted my ear and head scratches willingly. Soon, I had him eating an apple out of my hand, and not long after, Samuel helped me into the saddle.

To start with, Samuel had Don trail his horse. Still struggling to stay upright atop the boar, I didn't have it in me to direct him. Once the gates were open, the goats started running after us. They frolicked and bounced downhill as we led them away from the farm's enclosed spaces. Then, the males broke into a race.

"Once they beat each other, they'll try to outrun us," Samuel said. "It's roundabout now I start playing my flute."

"I can't possibly play my guitar and ride at the same time!" I protested.

"Da said you're a Journeyman. Playing your instrument should come second nature to you. So, focus on your riding and let your hands do what comes naturally to them."

I tried following Samuel's advice, but it was easier said than done. Keeping my hand on the fretboard proved difficult. I kept having to let go to grasp Don's reins.

"Put your trust in Don," Samuel said. "He's a good boar. The last thing he wants is for you to fall off. Grip his sides with your knees and feet, and play a damned song. We'll be out late if the bucks manage to get away."

Inhaling deeply, I closed my eyes. With Samuel's horse guiding Don, I had little to worry about. So, clearing my mind of worry, I played a soft melody. I did it more for myself at first. It helped me calm my racing heart and get over the nervousness of riding for the first time.

⌈ **Riding Mastery, unlocked!**
You're no Blood Rider, but at least you're not falling out of the saddle.
Riding Novice: Rank 1

⌋

The notification gave me the confidence boost I needed.

"Quick!" Samuel yelled. "If they get out of earshot, your song will do no good."

He didn't need to tell me twice. Now that I had the Mastery, I didn't feel as shaky anymore. In fact, the wind blowing through my hair felt brilliant. So, instead of playing one of my songs, I picked Free Bird. It felt appropriate with my hair flying all over the place—I could get used to riding.

Seeing the goats calm down en masse sent shivers down my spine. It took two whole verses, but I did that. The charging bucks slowed and fell into line with the rest of the flock, and Curry used the opportunity to catch up to the male kids; his legs weren't as long as theirs.

We crested the hill to find a giant field of tall grass ahead of us. Hilly woodland bordered it, cutting off my view of the horizon. Following Samuel's instructions, I stopped playing, and we let the goats spread out into the field.

"Aren't you worried they'll wander into the woods?" I asked after dismounting. The goats divided themselves into little cliques. One of the bucks immediately made his way to a mound near the treeline. He was so far away I doubted he'd heard my music from where I stood.

"In the wild, lead bucks aren't used to competing males in the herd. Here, we have six of similar physical prowess. If we weren't here to stop them, they might fight each other to death for the right to rule. Da says, usually, the weaker ones hang back, mating with the leader's rejects and help defend against predators, but will never challenge their leader," Samuel's eyes lit up as he prefaced his answer with an explanation. I guessed he didn't get to chat with others on the farm. "The bucks might get curious, but they don't trust each other to watch the flock. The nannies all have kids. So, they know better than to venture near the woods. Once in a while, one of the younger ones might wander away, but that's why we're here. Besides, breaking up fights that's pretty much all you've got to worry about."

"Then why do we have a pike and bow?"

"Wolves," he answered. "Once in a while, when they have trouble finding game, the packs will wander east looking for livestock. A couple of times every few months they'll test the waters, but we've not had a proper attack in years." We headed over to the large tree on the hill. Its shade gave us some respite from the hot mid-morning sun, while the elevation let us keep an eye on the whole flock and our mounts at the same time. "Enough of that. It's my turn to ask questions. The collars are enough to see us through my sniffles, and Da isn't a fan of bringing in outside help. Where are you from, and where are you headed?"

"You're direct, aren't you?" I laughed unsure whether to answer him honestly or not. Thinking back, Walter seemed to know what had happened in Blacknail's Table; I didn't want to get caught in a lie. "I'm just a man trying to make something of myself, that's all. In all honesty, I spent most of my life in relative safety, unsure of what I want to do with my future. I did what I was told to do, and that was that. Now that I have the freedom to decide, I don't know what I want from life."

"You're hoping to find your way in Eldar's Port, then?"

"That's the plan."

"It's not the best of places right now," Samuel said. "There's a lot of friction between the Merchant's Guild and the people."

"Yes, your father was telling me about that," I replied. "I'm hoping to stay away from all of that. I just want to find some Bardic or Arcane Training, maybe an apprenticeship. Escaping the cappers taught me I don't know enough of the world to make something of myself. Eldar's Port might be a mess, but I have to start somewhere."

Then, I heard a clip-clop behind me. I recognised it straight away but was too slow to attack. Curry headbutted me in the back for the second time in one day. I jumped to my feet, with a fist pulled back, and the kid looked back at me with a challenging stare.

"No," I told myself when the urge to smack him reared its vengeful head. Breathing deeply helped me stay in control until I no longer saw red. "Is he going to grow out of that?"

"He's not going to get the chance to," Samuel said, reminding me of Curry's destiny. "Most kids don't have the issue."

"I can see why you named him Curry." Looking into the goat's eyes, I poked his snout. "I've never eaten goat, and until now, I never planned to. For this asshole of a kid, I think I'll make an exception. How old is he?"

"Just under a year. We try to decide between keeping a buck before they're twelve, at most fifteen months old. After that, they don't count as kids anymore, and most butchers shy away from adult goat meat on account of its toughness."

"Do the kids sell well?"

"Our cattle fetch a premium most of the time," Samuel replied with a hint of pride in his voice. "However, last season, sales were poor. So, Da is branching out a little. He rarely goes as far as Hunter's Watch. At least this time he sold almost all of what he took with him."

I didn't like the look in Curry's eyes as he backed away. Seeing my reaction, Samuel started chuckling but didn't come to my aid. We both knew what was happening. In an attempt to evade Curry, I ran around the tree. Much to my disappointment, he had his mind set and took a running start. When the kid knocked me down again, Samuel burst into laughter. I, on the other hand, didn't think it funny. By bedtime, I'd be covered in bruises.

CHAPTER 26
IT'S THE THRILL OF THE FIGHT

After a week on the farm, Samuel and I developed a good working rhythm and fell into a routine. Walter and his helper, Joe, would wake up before us and milk the goats. Once they finished, Walter would head out with his cart. Then, we would let the goats out and do our morning chores: leading them out to the pastures and bringing them back before sunset. While we were out, Joe would fill the feeding troughs. According to Samuel, the grass wasn't sufficient food for milk-giving goats, and the male kids needed special diets to improve the flavour of their meat. Walter and Samuel took pride in their product and invested a lot of coin in their livestock.

When out in the pastures, I would have to keep an eye out for Curry's headbutts. He still managed to get me a couple of times every day, but I managed to evade a good deal of them. Walter expressed his frustration with the kid. Not only was he a handful, but no one would pay the asking price of twenty silver for the runt. Apparently, it was half of what he got for the other male goats. If no one bought him following the trip to Eldar's Port, Walter planned on slaughtering Curry himself and curing the meat for winter.

During my second week, I noticed something off while the goats were out grazing. Usually, the billies would stick to their section of the fields and occasionally come together to butt heads. It only got out of hand a couple of times, and I settled the matter quickly with a couple of songs. Now, they had all huddled together. The youngest kids got pushed into the middle, with the females in a ring around them. The older male kids stood near the outside of the circle. The billies stood close to each other facing the woods, bleating loudly and stamping the ground beneath them.

"Samuel, the goats are acting weird," I said, shaking the slumbering goatherd.

"They're goats," he replied, batting my hand away. "They're weird by nature."

"Not like this, mate. I think there's something in the woods scaring them."

He jumped onto his feet straight away and scanned the treeline. The billies were now kicking up chunks of earth and bobbing their horned heads up and down. It looked like they were threatening to charge. Samuel whistled. His horse came over trotting and Don followed hot on the mare's tail. Despite the species difference, the pair had made their love for each other clear during the week. When left to their own devices, the couple followed each other getting up to no good. Unnatural and disturbing, but supposedly very common on a farm.

Samuel hopped onto his horse and fumbled with his bow as he tried to string it. "Play something mellow," he told me. "We can't let the bucks rile themselves up. We need them to be calm."

"Will you tell me what's going on, first?"

"Wolves."

"What manner of wolves can take these monsters down? Look at them. They're huge!"

"Just play a damned song!"hHe barked, making me jump. "If a billie charges, he's not going to stop until he hits something or is out of breath, and Nil Mountain Goats don't easily get out of breath." He calmed, noticing my wide eyes and erratic breathing. I had warned them about my dislike of violence. "These aren't ordinary wolves. As long as the flock is together, everything should be fine; but if one of the billies gets into the woods, the wolves will swarm him with ease. Then, there will be a hole in the flock's defence, and we'll have panicked kids running amok, getting trampled."

I didn't waste any time on song selection. The wind had picked up, and I worried how far the sound would carry. So, something slow was out of the question. I picked a melody with a steady tempo and loud chorus. One of my own, of course. Still, the bucks didn't settle. They were too far away.

Despite Samuel's protests, I hopped on Don's back and rode downhill. Walter hired me for a job, and I intended to see it done to the best of my abilities. I stopped near the foothill when the billies stopped stamping their hooves, tearing up the grass and soil underneath. Still, they kept their guard up. Now calmed, they didn't let rage or fear cloud their judgement.

Samuel was right. The goats deserved more credit. The billies spread out more evenly and the male kids filled in the gaps between them. Now the flock had a proper line of defence between them and the woods. I didn't stop playing. Instead, I moved on to a more upbeat song, 'We are the Champions'. I couldn't be sure whether the song's tone made a difference or not, but I wanted to promote unity among the goats.

"You better keep on fighting or it's going to be the end," I sang, making the lyrics my own. Sorry for butchering your lyrics, Freddy Mercury. If jovians can grow moustaches, I'll nurture one in your honour.

Since he had a higher Perception score than me, Samuel saw the wolves first. Nocking an arrow, he rode up to the head of the flock. I saw a sharp focus in his eyes that didn't suit the man I had befriended over the last week. Samuel drew his bow and loosed. His arrow flew into the woods, and we heard a yelp from within the darkness. He had another arrow nocked moments later.

Half a dozen wolves came running out of the woods together. Samuel wasn't kidding around. The monsters put Earth's wolves to shame. The canines weren't just twice as big, but had sabretooth-tiger-like fangs as well. They broke into two groups after nearing the flock and ran in opposite directions looking for a weak link in the vanguard. Samuel quickly put an arrow in the closest wolf's left eye. It yelped falling back. The billies charged forward, interrupting the remaining wolves' sprint. But counter to what Samuel said before, they returned to the defensive encirclement instead of carrying on into the woods. My take on Freddy's lyrics and melody had turned them into champions after all.

Don grunted shuffling to the side. Following his gaze, I spotted a lone wolf emerging from the trees to my right. It had its eyes trained on me. Unlike Samuel and his horse, Don and I were not one with the flock. Targeting me made sense.

I didn't dare stop playing my song. If the goats fell into disarray, things could potentially get ugly. Instead, I instinctively dug my heels into Don's side. With a surprised squeal, he ran towards the assembled goats. The wolf went from careful stalking to sprint straight away. We weren't going to make it. I could tell. The wolf would catch up to us before we reached the flock. Still, I wasn't ready to give up.

A loud crack and a yelp sounded from where the bucks made their stand. One of them had managed to catch a big, brown wolf in his charge. The sound made our pursuer jump, but moments later it continued its chase. With every heartbeat, he got closer. I considered dropping Diya and picking up the pike. Don could carry me while I suffered the debuff, but then, the goats might go wild. Without their tight formation, the wolves would probably pick off stragglers and take several kids as their prize.

I tried to regulate my breathing and slow my racing heart, but with the wolf hot on my tail, my efforts proved fruitless. On Earth, I used to call myself a dog person; in my new reality, not so much. I expected my race and traits to make me less of a target, but clearly, there was a lot more to **Game World** that I didn't understand. I was moments from reaching the flock when I heard a loud crack and yelp behind me. Don, skid to a halt without my prompting, almost throwing me off his back. We turned around. Curry had charged the monster. The annoying bugger had saved me!

The wolf was getting back on its feet. He wasn't done. I guessed Curry lacked the bulk to finish it in one blow. Screw it. I had played my guitar just fine with five Control. I could probably do it with half a unit less than that.

Over the last week, I had raised my Riding Mastery to the fourth Novice rank. Samuel called my growth rate 'too damn high'. Turning Don around, I had the boar charge at the canine and switched to playing 'Eye of the Tiger'—I did skip the long intro though. My current situation didn't allow for it. Much to my surprise, knocking the wolf down didn't earn me the debuff. So, even though I made Don execute the attack, it didn't count as me directly hurting someone.

Then, Curry turned and charged at the down wolf again. It snapped at his legs when he approached, but the kid skidded to the halt before reaching the beast. Instead, he raised himself up onto his hind legs and stamped down on the wolf's head with both hooves. My stomach churned, hearing the loud crunch.

The entire herd advanced in unison. They didn't charge but moved forward as one. The wolves slowed, looking between one another and the trees behind them.

"Keep playing that song," Samuel yelled. "I've never seen the flock behave this way before!"

Nodding, I sang as loud as I could, "It's the eye of the goat; it's the thrill of the fight!" man, I don't know why I changed the words. The goats didn't very well understand the lyrics.

Excluding the beast that had come for me, four wolves were dead. Out of arrows, Samuel levelled his pike like a lance, couching it between his underarm, and charged at the closest canine. Then, a spine-chilling howl sounded from within the woodland's darkness.

I held my breath, expecting more wolves to appear out of the trees, but none came. The two surviving members of the daring pack turned and ran back towards the treeline. Samuel didn't give up his chase and managed to get a glancing blow on his target's rear leg. It barked in pain but still managed to escape.

Turning his horse around, Samuel rode towards me and pointed up the hill. Understanding what he meant, I nodded. Dropping 'Eye of the Tiger', I picked up a sombre melody of my design and within the next minute, the goats followed. Though dusk was still several hours away, we started our trip back to the farm.

"My heart won't stop racing," I said, as we followed the herd. After the attack, the herd didn't need guidance and stuck to the practised path. My music helped, of course, but after my week of playing for them, I understood it didn't take away their free will altogether. "How do you manage that alone?"

"I don't," he answered. "Often Da or Joe join me on my outings. Today was something else. Even with me on the flute, the flock never behaves the way they did. Not only were they calm, but the bucks were communicating and coordinating with one another."

"I'm as impressed as you. The defensive encirclement they formed was as good as a military formation."

"How did you get Curry to take down a wolf? He's just a kid! None of his brothers left the circle."

"I didn't do anything," I told him. Curry stuck close to Don's side as we made our journey back. "For a moment, I was sure Don and I were done for. Bloody hell, I didn't even see it happen, mate. Just heard a loud crunch and I knew something had taken the bastard down."

"Da will be impressed. We never get away from an attack this clean. The reason we keep six bucks is that there is always the danger of losing one to an attack. Sometimes, if they suffer a grave injury, we have no option besides putting them down. It's cheaper to lose an animal or two than to hire proper protection."

"So, what's going to happen now? To the wolves, I mean."

"They never venture far from the woods," Samuel explained. "The pack will test a couple other dairy farmers in the area; they mostly keep sheep and cows. While their herds are easier to manage than ours, they aren't as threatening as our goats. The wolves might pick off enough for a meal, and then they'll return to their home turf. They've been trying to expand their territory for years, but we farmers keep each other informed. As long as we're around, it's never going to happen."

I didn't stop playing until the goats crossed the threshold into Walter's land, and Samuel closed the gate behind us. Some of the flock headed straight into the barn, but most remained in the field. My entire body ached from the day's excitement. Hopping off Don, I had a good stretch, taking pleasure in the sound of my joints popping.

Then, Curry rammed me from behind knocking me down. Frustrated, I jumped to my feet and looked the kid in the eye. "I've had it with you," I yelled in its face. Samuel looked at me, amused as he took the saddle off my boar mount. "Fine, you saved me, but why in the world do you keep headbutting me?!"

Curry looked at me quizzically, clearly not understanding the reason for my anger. His horns had grown since I first saw him. They were little more than stubs now, but still not the majestic black horns the mature bucks displayed. Once those grew in, his charges would hurt. I hoped to be gone by then. I'd be happy never seeing the beast ever again.

I recognised the look in Curry's eyes as he hopped backwards. The kid planned on headbutting me again. Screw it. If he wanted someone to butt heads with that bad, I decided to give him what he wanted. Maybe then he'd leave me alone. Angling my head down, I bashed my skull against his just as he hopped forward to boop me. I regretted my decision immediately.

> You have violated the Pacifist Trait's commandment. All stats have been halved until you get a full night of undisturbed sleep.

The world had gone blurry. My jelly knees gave way under me, and my head bounced off packed earth. I caught a glimpse of Curry and Samuel looking down at me through the floating blue screen before everything turned black.

Chapter 27
I Ain't Afraid of No Goat

The sun's rays woke me up. How long had I been out? We were still hours from sunset when we got back to the farm. Samuel must have carried me to bed. I peeked out the window. It was midday, the barn doors were open and the goats weren't in sight. I had slept through the evening, night and morning.

I touched my forehead—no bump, bruise, or pain. Of course. **Game World** likely had magic or potions to fix welts and concussions, but considering how long it had taken me to recover, I guessed the injury must have been a major one. Unlike Curry, my skull wasn't exactly made for bashing.

Several notifications blinked in my peripheral vision, demanding my attention. Right, I recalled brushing them away during the wolf attack.

> Look at you taking risks!
> Big things do come in little packages, after all. Riding Mastery has progressed to Novice: Rank 7

I didn't have a metric for comparison, and my race description didn't specify a number for the bonus growth rates, but I thought it safe to assume they increased at least twice as fast than the standard. I still needed three more ranks until I got any bonus stats from it, so I swiped left.

> Curry, the young Nil Mountain Goat, has forever spent his life rejected by his peers. By giving him the acknowledgement he so desperately wanted, you have tamed him. Congratulations!
> As the first resident of Game World to tame a Nil Mountain Goat, you've attracted divine attention. Demi, Deity of Harvest and Floods sends you and your new companion gifts.

Beast Taming Mastery unlocked!
Beast Taming Mastery has progressed to Apprentice: Rank 5
    Brawn + 1
    Mind + 1
    Charisma + 1

Achievement Unlocked!
Hard Headed
    Charisma + 2

You have one unassigned stat point.
Curry gains bonus Trait: Natural Beast of Burden.

A bleat made me jump. Looking past the screen, I saw Curry watching me through the window. He probably refused to follow Samuel out to the pasture. I read through the notifications again—damn stupid reason for awarding someone an achievement. Bloody hell, I could have died! I needed to get my impulses under control. Surely, there had to be a better way to progress in this world.

I wondered whether I would have earned these bonuses if not for Maka's introduction to the stern woman. Closing my eyes, I could almost picture her calling me Hard Headed. Still, though unadvisable, the act had provided me with significant growth. After adding the extra point to Charisma, I checked my character sheet.

Identification:
    First Name: Peregrin   Last Name: Kanooks
    Race: Jovian   Patron:—
    Condition: Healthy   Mana Core: Full
Stats:
    Brawn: 2   Control: 8
    Mind: 4   Arcana: 1
    Charisma: 19   Perception: 8

Traits:
  Pacifist
  Facts Begin With Fiction
  Arcane Chords

Underwhelming. My flexed bicep didn't look any bigger. I didn't feel any stronger or cognitively superior than I did before. So, the stat growth wasn't cumulative. If only the system were like the RPGs, I grew up playing. My new world probably didn't have any formulas to help me figure out numbers like damage, health or armour.

Then again, could any reality really work off such values?

Oh no! Somebody stabbed me, my health went down by five points!

I'm level hundred! Your arrow to the knee can't penetrate my still human skin!

I slashed you with my dagger of dumbfuckery! Now you've suffered sixty-nine points of damage.

The lack of levels made me happy. They didn't make any sense in a real-world scenario. Come to think of it, damage and health would mean nothing to me either way. Given the road I planned on walking, attacking anyone would result in my death. Letting anyone hit me would probably end similarly.

I owed Maka my thanks. If not for her, Demi probably wouldn't be watching me.

Curry bleated once again. He wanted my attention. After changing into a fresh set of clothes, I pulled on Gram's cloak and exited the farmhouse. Curry came prancing over. Instead of headbutting me, the kid pressed his forehead against mine gently. When I reached out to pet him, he didn't pull away.

"Joe?" I yelled, stroking Curry's snout.

No answer. The farmhand must have accompanied Samuel. Probably for the best. If the wolves were still in the area, going back alone wouldn't end well. Besides, no way in hell was I going to fight for my life two days in a row. I'd rather shovel shit than deal with that stress.

Curry rubbed his head against my outstretched hand, so I stroked him some more. Then, I felt something brushing against my leg. Looking down, I saw Boots. Was she watching over me? Or, was she only paying attention because I was sharing my affection with another animal? I could've used her help the day before or when Gor hatched a plan to use me as worm feed.

Looking up, she meowed at me. I picked her up to give the feline cosmic messenger the attention she wanted only for Curry to nudge me with his head and bleat loudly in my ear. Okay. If Beast Taming involved entertaining several needy beings, it wasn't going to be as fun as I thought.

I wondered whether the Devourer of Worlds knew her former herald was visiting me. If she did, how did she feel about it? I wanted her to notice me, but not anytime soon. First, I needed to make something out of myself.

Reaching up with a paw, Boots swatted my face.

"What is it?" I asked her.

My Mastery menu popped up in front of my eyes. Boots meowed again, and the Beast Taming Mastery highlighted itself. The cat looked between me and the screen. How powerful an entity was she? Could all higher beings manipulate my user interface? If I weren't so used to cats, I'd think of it as a major invasion of my privacy. However, curiosity got the better of me, and I wanted to know what Boots was getting at.

I selected the Mastery, and a pets menu showed up. It only had one tab, labelled Curry.

⌠ **Name: Curry**
Race: Nil Mountain Goat (Youngling)
Age: 11 months
Major Focus: Brawn
Minor Focus: Arcana
**Description: Due to several millennia of living in the Null

Mountain Region, they're a hardier species than most. Nil Mountain Goats have three interests in life: food, caring for their flock, and fighting. They grow up locking horns with one another until a single male earns the role of alpha which he will furiously protect to the death.
Traits:
    Natural Beast of Burden
    \<Unassigned\>
    \<Unassigned\>

Minor focus Arcana? Curry could develop magical abilities! I take it back. Beast Taming would pair brilliantly with Charisma as long as I found more weird-ass beasts like him. I found the Traits category interesting as well. Unfortunately, a Familiar voice interrupted me before I could investigate.

"We need to talk, Master Kanooks," Walter called, walking towards with a sterner than usual look on his face. When he called me by my last name instead of Perry, I knew something wasn't right straight away.

"Good morning, Walter." I waved at him, feeling like a schoolboy summoned to the principal's office. "I'm sorry I didn't get to my chores this morning. I'll start on whatever is left right now."

"You took a blow to the head. Give the healing brew time to do its job. You're not working today. In fact, I'm not sure whether you'll be working for us at all."

"What? I'm sorry, I don't know what Samuel told you, but I did the best I could yesterday." My heart dropped. Besides the wolf attack, I had started enjoying my work. Sure, I knew the gig had an expiration date, but I didn't think it would come so soon.

"It's not that, Samuel doesn't even know about this." When Walter let out a heavy sigh, I knew it was a done deal. He had already made up his mind. "I'm guessing you're not familiar with running an operation of this kind. The system provides a special interface to help with management, stock taking and general logistics. It shows you tamed one of my livestock. Not only is that a major breach of my trust, but you've also done what generations of my family have been unable to do. You have no idea how frustrating that is."

"Walter, I didn't mean to. I promise. I told you, I didn't even have the Beast Taming Mastery until now." Curry bleated loudly at Walter, making me jump. It was then I realised, Boots had disappeared out of my hands without me noticing. "He kept headbutting me, I got pissed off and did it back to him. That's all I did. Then, I wake up this morning, and the system tells me I've tamed him."

Walter stared at me long and hard, probably thinking I was lying. Walking over to Curry, he pulled a hand-sized metal rod out of his pocket. My heart leapt into my chest, thinking he intended to slaughter the kid in front of me. Not long ago, I hated the beast and wanted it dead. I don't know whether it was the taming or because he let me pet him, but all of a sudden, I felt an emotional connection to Curry.

"Please don't kill him," I begged. "I don't know how, but there has to be a way to transfer the companionship to you. I'm sure people sell tamed animals all the time. I know Curry is small but look at his hooves. I don't know if its the same for goats but my father used to say, 'bigger the paws, bigger the dog,' I'm sure he'll grow into a mighty buck."

"I'm not going to kill him, boy." Walter burst out laughing. He pressed the cylinder to Curry's neck and a thin ring of metal popped open. I hadn't seen it under the thick goat hair. "He was no good to me before, he's no use to me now. I'm docking your week's pay, and you're free to do whatever you want with the kid."

"So, I still have a job?" I asked, my face lighting up.

"Heavens, no! I don't want you taming anymore of my livestock on accident or on purpose. You're out. Eldar's Port is a day and a half away, and I saw the strange trait Curry unlocked. You can ride him there." He said, pocketing the collar. Walter tried petting Curry, but he hopped away from his former owner. "You don't have to tell me the truth about how you did it either. I don't want my son or Joe risking their lives headbutting these giant assholes. What were you even thinking, doing that? You're a jovian. You could have died!"

I didn't bother trying to change Walter's mind. He'd already made his decision. At least, I was now close to my destination and no longer alone. I thought it rather fitting that my first friend in the strange new world was a goat. Life couldn't just be easy and give me a cat, dog, or even a mouse. It had to be a behemoth goat that used its head to solve life's problems. Literally.

Epilogue

Little Capper, Big Capper

The rain came as a relief to Sloane and Hruk. Over a week had passed since they descended the mountains and escaped Blacknail's Table, but they still couldn't dodge the warg riders. Hruk wasn't surprised. His father and brother—may the spirits embrace them—used to raise wargs for a living. He knew how adept at tracking their keen noses made them. Now, hopefully, the rain would wash away any tracks Sloane and he left behind.

If the stupid human had caved in Swamp Brorc shit as he had, they would've lost the wargs long ago. Every child in Blacknail's Table and the Bracken Swamps knew few smells could repel a warg, and the porcine beasts' odour was one of them. Sloane had refused to do it. The scrimshaw said if he died, he wanted to do so with dignity. Stupid human.

Hruk wasn't just any capper. He'd been born the smallest of his generation. Despite his father's attempts at cleansing the bloodline, Hruk had reached adulthood just fine. Sure. He wouldn't have made it there if not for his willingness to do whatever it took to survive; but he didn't expect Sloane to understand. Hruk just hoped the human's stubbornness wouldn't get him killed.

"We need to go west," Sloane said. "If the swamps start flooding, we'll be in a whole lot of trouble."

"But that'll take us further away from Eldar's Port!" Hruk protested. "We need to wait a while longer—"

"They're not coming, Hruk. The sooner you get that, the better." Sloane had been repeating the same thing for several days now. Hruk didn't want to believe him at first, but now he wasn't so sure any more. "Perry either got captured, or the wargs chased them in another direction.

We can head south, but I can't guarantee your survival. It's not as bad to the west." Sloane tapped his bone staff. "I can protect you there."

"Then what? The plan was we stick together!" Hruk had hoped Perry would help him find his kink, perhaps someone that had a fetish for small, skinny cappers with smooth, baby-like skin. Capper women liked it rough, and he was far from it—figuratively and literally. "Perry and I planned to travel together."

"Well, Hruk, plans change." Sloane sighed. Hruk knew the human had no obligations towards him. If he wanted, Sloane could abandon the skinny capper and go his own way. "Tell you what. Once we get to a decent town, I'll help you get some work. Once you've earned some money, you can take a riverboat to Eldar's Port. How's that sound?"

"Acceptable," Hruk said after some thought. He'd rendezvous with Perry eventually. The jovian would teach him all about kinks and fetishes, and then life would be good. Hruk had put a lot of thought into what kind of woman he hoped had a kink for him. He wanted someone tall; not capper tall, but wood aelph tall. Big breasts were compulsory. On second thought, big breasts would do; he wasn't too picky. They didn't even have to be the same size. He belonged to the school of thought that all breasts were beautiful. He had always dreamed of having a heavy breast rest on his face, and you'd need something decent-sized for that.

Sooner or later he'd find Perry. Before meeting the jovian, Hruk had given up on life, let alone finding happiness. He didn't know what it was, but there was something different about Perry. The capper had hope for the future now. He had a purpose.

Howls snapped the pair to attention.

"We should get moving," Sloane said, getting up. "If we can get far enough before the rain picks up, they'll never find us."

"No. We need to hide." That's right. After meeting Perry, Hruk had found his voice as well. "Their sense of smell might be confused now, but until it starts pouring, they can track us by ear," he explained. "Besides, the mud might slow us down, but the warg riders will be in their element. With all the boulders and fallen trees everywhere, the wargs won't touch the ground until they're right above us."

After Hruk helped them escape the riders twice, Sloane had learned to trust him. They crept out of their hiding place, doing their best to avoid muddy patches and twigs. One misstep would give away their position. Hruk's heart threatened to beat out of his chest.

Sloane's staff struck a hollow tree trunk, and the woods around them went silent. Hruk didn't give it a second thought and started running. Sloane followed after a moment's hesitation. A howl sounded not far behind them, and several others sounded not far away. After all his big talk, it was the stupid human that gave them away. Hruk had survived his family, he had survived wrongful imprisonment, and now he'd survive this too.

"Keep up!" Hruk hissed as Sloane struggled with the mud. His light frame came in handy for once. The capper had little trouble using hollow logs and unstable stones for footholds. Unfortunately, they sunk under Sloane's weight and he fell further behind with each footstep.

Hruk needed to do something quickly, or Sloane would get killed. Going forward, Hruk knew he needed the human to survive. Even if he got to a settlement, people would take one look at him and write him off as a thief. No one would hire him for physical jobs either. As much as Hruk wanted to deny it, perhaps his father was right. Pursuing a career as a scribe had been a wasted effort.

Brawn had never been his strong suit. Hruk compensated with loads of Control, Mind, and Perception. He snatched a small stone off the ground and spun on his heel. The warg and its rider were almost upon them. They stood atop a tall boulder, preparing to pounce on Sloane. For a moment, his eyes met the riders. They knew each other; not long ago, the bigger capper had bullied him and shoved him around at Klinkle's. By the spirits, the bastard had made fun out of Perry too.

Hruk hadn't attacked anyone since his imprisonment. He remembered the day like it were yesterday—ignore the cliche. The shaman's son had recently joined the warg riders. The young capper had bullied Hruk since they were children, and now the sadist had power over him once again. For weeks, he put up with the shaman's son. He'd long learnt to ignore the torment and just focus on the job on hand. However, things changed when the young capper dropped Hruk in a hole full of warg shit and blocked the exit with a weighted plank of wood.

After almost freezing to death and scrubbing himself raw to wash off the scent, Hruk found himself on a path to vengeance. He waited until the hunters returned from a hunt with a trio of warg pups. As expected, the shaman's son had inherited his father's pride. Despite his inexperience, he used his influence for the right to break and tame a new warg. When no one was watching, Hruk stole a chunk of liver from the kitchen and slipped it into his foe's pocket.

The young capper survived, but the warg pup mangled his legs, leaving him a cripple. Hruk got caught with bloody fingers, and he had a motive. As a result, he didn't get away with his crime. Now that he faced another bully, Hruk channelled all the rage and contempt he had bottled away over the years. He threw his rock, and it flew straight into the warg rider's eye. The capper screamed, falling from his saddle, and the spirits sided with Hruk. Thunder struck, masking the sound, as well as the warg's whining in response to his blinded master's pain. The drizzle turned into a downpour so heavy, he could barely see Sloane behind him.

"C'mon!" Hruk yelled, running back to help the human out of the mud. With a little heaving, he got Sloane free. "Hold my hand," he told him. "So we don't get separated."

Sloane went a step further. He lifted the Capper onto his shoulders and ran towards higher ground. Following Hruk's directions, Sloane only stepped wherever dense roots kept the ground stable. The pair decided they'd risk tripping over getting stuck again. Warg riders were the hardiest among the Cappers. Their pursuers would recover, regroup, and they'd find them despite the rain. They needed to hide. Hruk desperately wanted to hide.

"There," he said into Sloane's ear, pointing at a thicket of trees ahead. "We'll look for a hollow there."

"Are you sure about this?" Sloane asked. Hruk could barely hear the human over the heavy rain.

"Trust me. I've run from them all my life. The riders will expect us to keep running."

The pair ran into the trees. With or without the rain, they'd be near impossible to find among the thick trunks. Sloane slowed as the pair scanned for a good hiding place. They needed a spot that would protect them from the rain as well. Hruk saw nothing during his initial scan. Since he had a higher Perception score, he took it upon himself to find shelter. At the thicket's centre sat a tree as thick as a warg was long. Hruk did a double-take when he saw its bark shifting and morphing.

"There!" He pointed as a small opening appeared on its trunk.

Sloane nodded, running over to it. Hruk scrambled down the man's back and slipped into the opening. Sloane followed. Unfortunately, neither got the respite they were looking for. Instead of solid ground, the hole housed a muddy hole, and the pair found themselves sliding down it into darkness.

Hruk landed in a pool of wet sludge. It splashed all over his face, blinding him. Unlike Sloan, he managed to stay upright.

"Are you okay?" Hruk asked, feeling around blindly for his companion.

He found Sloane. The human didn't respond to his prodding. Hruk pressed an ear to his companion's chest. He heard a heartbeat. Sloane was breathing too. The sludge was shallow enough for the capper to stand in but had sufficient depth to drown the human. Though still blind, Hruk dragged Sloane until he felt them moving up an incline and away from the pool of viscous fluid.

The capper's jaw dropped when he finally wiped the gunk out of his eyes. Instead of a cave, he found himself standing in a green clearing bathed in sunlight. "Wake up," he said, shaking and slapping Sloane. "You need to see this, stupid man."

Hruk's mouth started salivating when he saw the fruit-laden tree in front of him. Best of all, he didn't need to climb to get the almost golden pears. A handful lay on the ground in front of him. The capper looked to his left and right as he approached it. His many years as the city's nobody had taught him when something felt too good to be true, it probably was.

"It's safe," a voice said, making him jump. "Don't worry."

Somehow he hadn't seen the beautiful wood aelph standing among the trees. Then he got a closer look. She didn't look like any wood aelph he'd seen before. There was something different about her. The light! She didn't need the sun's light. Her skin glowed with a golden sheen no different from the wood. She sauntered into the clearing stark naked.

"Don't eat my heart, please," he told her, backing away towards Sloane. His heartbeat had calmed for a moment, but the sight of her sent it racing again. He couldn't tell whether it was fear that triggered it, or her large breasts and wide swaying hips.

"Why would I do that?" she asked, laughing a hearty laugh. The trees around them shook in rhythm with her breasts.

"I've read about your kind: you're a dryad. Dryads lure men into their lair and eat their heart."

"Ah. I see how your kind could've misinterpreted that." She scooped a fruit from the ground and brushed the dirt of it with her long, golden fingers. A soft breeze blew through the clearing, making her chestnut hair dance. She took a bite out of the fruit before throwing it to Hruk. He snatched it out of the air reflexively. "I steal men's hearts in the more figurative sense. Once in a while, their wives get mad, murder their partners and blame it on me. I guess your interpretation can be true as well."

Hruk jumped when he felt something brush against his leg. It was a cat with orange fur and white markings around the feet. Now that he thought about it, he'd seen the feline in Blacknail's Table before. He recalled it sitting on a table in Klinkle's tavern just before Perry foolishly gave Lefa the Heart Tulip. It meowed, looking up at him.

"You don't have to repeat yourself, Miss Purrfect," the dryad said. "I promised, didn't I? They're safe. I won't turn them into my love slaves."

The term 'love slave' piqued Hruks interest. He looked between the naked woman and the cat. She ticked all his boxes. If she had a kink for him, he wouldn't mind living life being whatever she wanted him to be.

"Question is, are you willing to help him a bit more than that?" A disembodied voice asked. Unlike the dryad's, this one had an air of mischief to it. It reminded him of the aelf. Like the world was her plaything. "He's a friend of a friend. Investing in him will pay great dividends in the future."

A chill ran down Hruk's spine when he saw the voice's owner. A spider as big as his head crawled up from the dryad's back and perched itself on her shoulder. "Looking at your friends, I'm not sure whether I believe you or not," he said, feeling braver than his usual self. "I think I'd rather deal with the wargs out there."

The cat meowed, making the dryad and spider laugh. Fear was slowly winning the war against arousal. "I've already made up my mind," the dryad announced. "Allied to your friends or not, Hruk here is an interesting specimen."

"You know my name?"

"Now, I'll have to ask all unwanted guests to leave my grove." The dryad ignored him and waved at her unusual friends. She licked her fingers, and they disappeared. "Why won't you taste my fruit?" she asked, frowning at Hruk. "I picked that one, especially for you."

Unwilling to anger an entity as powerful as here. The capper caved and took a bite out of the pear. Its warm juices ran down his throat and warmed his stomach. Several notifications popped up in front of his eyes.

> You have partaken in a dryad's legendary fruit!
> All stats increased by 2.
> Achievement unlocked!
> Tree Hugger
>   Control + 1
>   Perception + 1
> You have an unassigned stat point.

"This tastes divine." Hruk gasped, brushing the notifications away. His fear melted away, only leaving arousal behind.

"You're an interesting specimen, Hruk," the dryad said. "You're smaller and skinnier than most of your kind, but you displayed amazing skill and courage to save your companion. On top of that, who's ever seen a capper scribe before.?"

The dryad moved in closer until their faces were almost touching. The capper felt her naked breasts press against his chest and Hruk was ready to go; he fulfilled the dryad's kink! Hruk couldn't wait to tell Perry about it.

"The written word and ancient runes have always intrigued me," the capper said, struggling to find his voice. If he weren't green, Hruk was sure his face would've turned red.

"So you do have an interest in magic?"

"Of course I do," he answered. "Every capper hopes to make a Covenant so they can speak to the spirits."

"What if I gave you wood-focused Manipulation instead?"

"I'd accept your gift without question. Magic is magic. I'm not stubborn like the shaman's followers. All arcane schools can help us reach the spirits."

The dryad took his hand and led him towards the clearing's centre. His eyes struggled to look away from her swaying hips. She sat on a soft mound and flowers bloomed around her. The glowing being of power took his hand, and pulled him down on top of her.

> A being of power has offered you a wood-focused Manipulation Attunement in exchange for your seed.
> Do you accept?

"By the spirits, yes!" Hruk exclaimed. An Attunement would help him reach Perry sooner. He couldn't wait to make the jovian jealous with tales of having his first time with a dryad.

Made in the USA
Monee, IL
27 January 2021